RAYMOND E. FEIST

JIMMY AND THE CRAWLER

HarperCollins*Publishers*
77–85 Fulham Palace Road,
Hammersmith, London W6 8JB

www.harpervoyagerbooks.com

Published by Harper*Voyager*
An imprint of HarperCollins*Publishers* 2013
1

A catalogue record for this book
is available from the British Library

ISBN: 978-0-00-751128-0

Set in Janson Text by Palimpsest Book Production Limited,
Falkirk, Stirlingshire

Printed and bound in Great Britain by
Clays Ltd, St Ives plc

To the gamers who bought *Betrayal at Krondor* and *Return to Krondor* and gave me an opportunity to work with some of my favourite characters again.

Acknowledgements

Besides my usual tip of the hat to the moms and dads of Midkemia, I'd like to add some people who were critical to the games upon which much of the Krondor series is based: John Cutter, Neal Halford, Bob Izrin, and St. John Bane. Without them, there would have been no *Betrayal at Krondor* or *Return to Krondor*. Along with these friends are the talented and dedicated people at Dynamix, 7th Level, and Pyrotechnix who put in killer hours to get out two fun games and give me nifty story elements to work with.

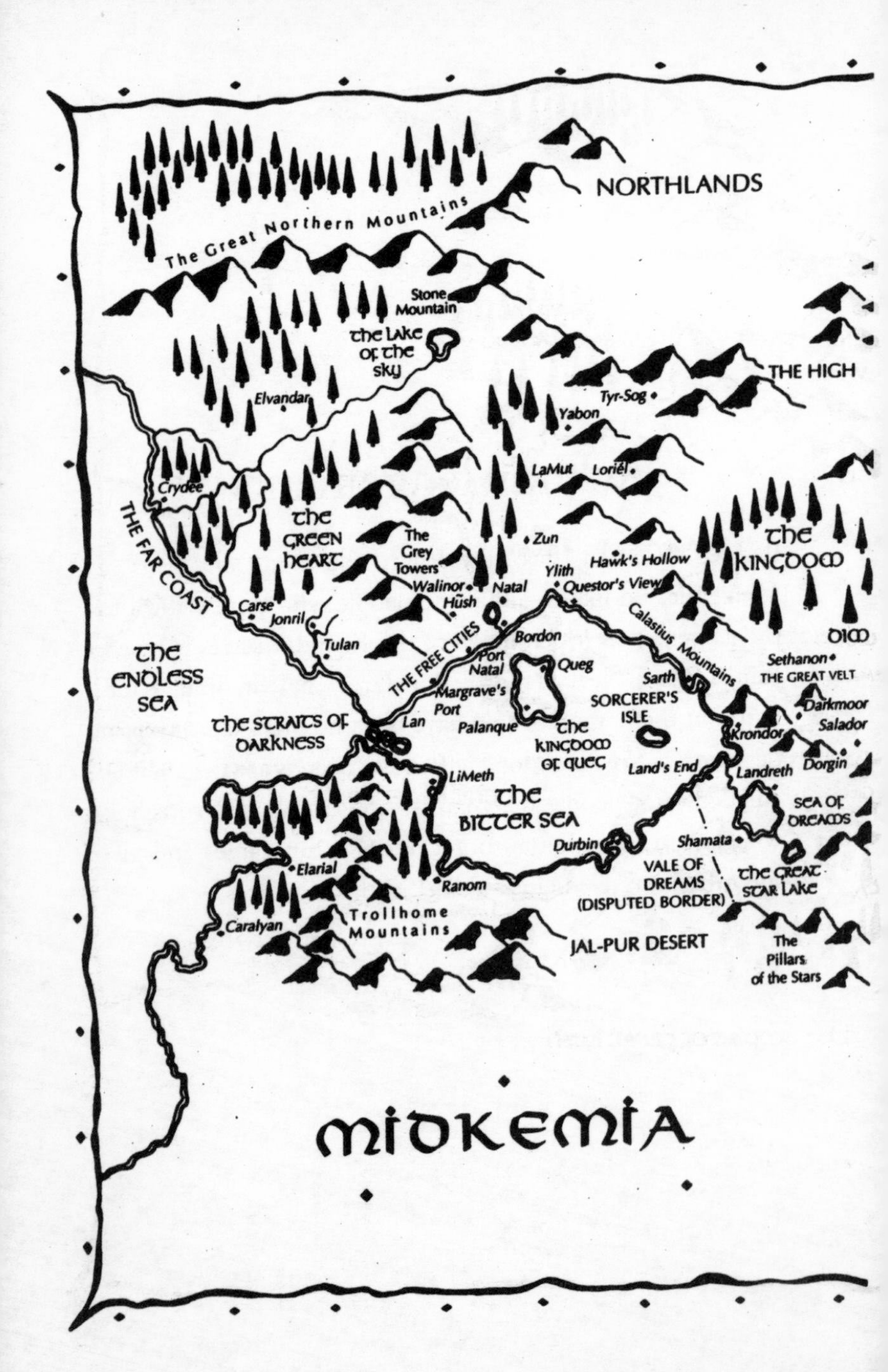
NORTHLANDS
The Great Northern Mountains
Stone Mountain
The Lake of the Sky
THE HIGH
Tyr-Sog
Yabon
Elvandar
LaMut
Loriél
Crydee
THE FAR COAST
The Green Heart
The Grey Towers
Zun
Hawk's Hollow
The Kingdom
Ylith
Questor's View
Walinor
Hūsh
Natal
Carse
Jonril
Tulan
THE FREE CITIES
Bordon
Port Natal
Calastius Mountains
The Endless Sea
Margrave's Port
Queg
Sarth
Sethanon
THE GREAT VELT
Darkmoor
Salador
Lan
Palanque
SORCERER'S ISLE
The Kingdom of Queg
The Straits of Darkness
Krondor
Dorgin
LiMeth
Land's End
Landreth
The Bitter Sea
SEA OF DREAMS
Durbin
Shamata
Elarial
Ranom
VALE OF DREAMS (DISPUTED BORDER)
The Great Star Lake
Trollhome Mountains
Caralyan
JAL-PUR DESERT
The Pillars of the Stars
MIDKEMIA

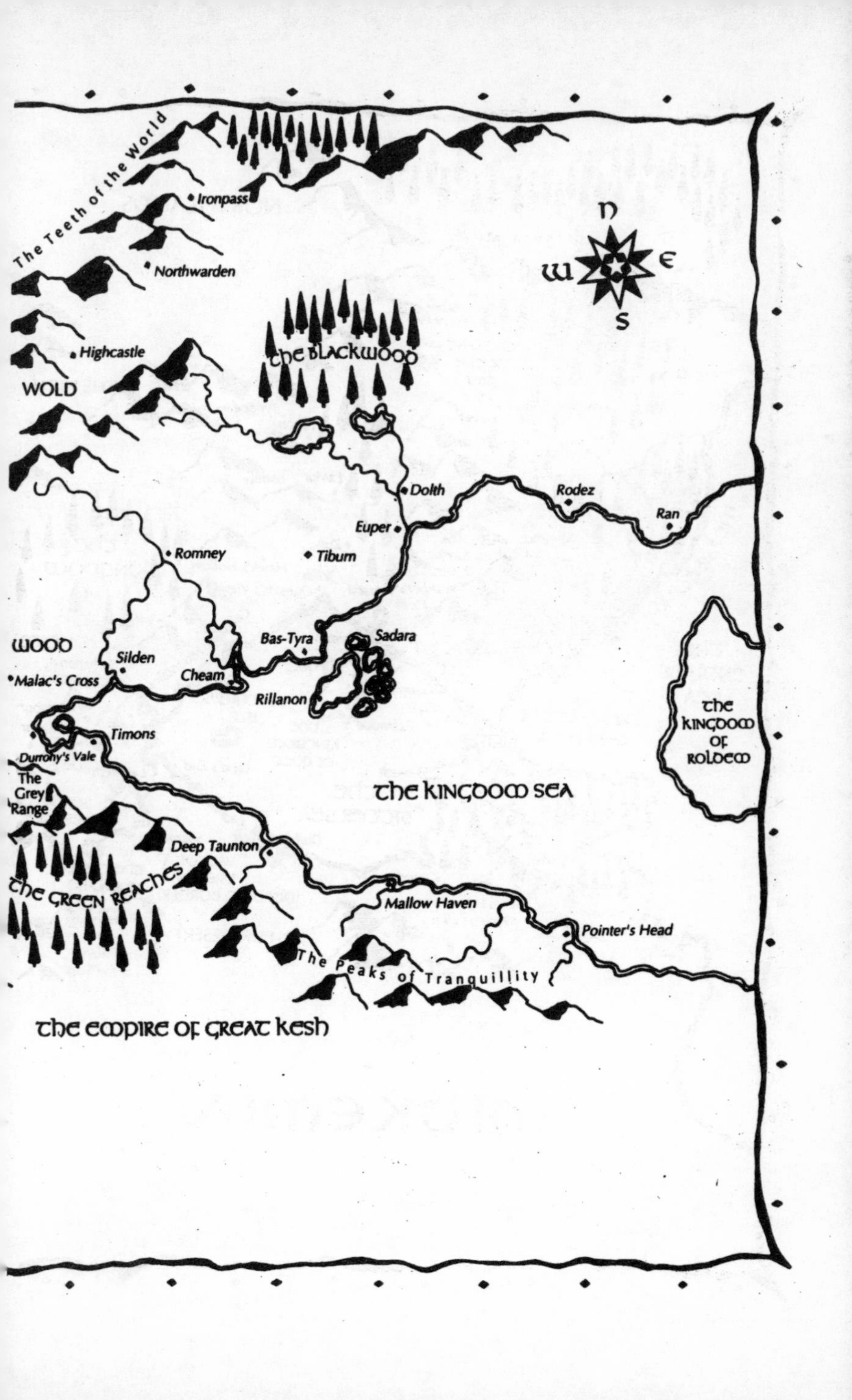
The Teeth of the World
Ironpass
Northwarden
Highcastle
WOLD
The Blackwood
N
W
E
S
Dolth
Rodez
Ran
Euper
Romney
Tiburn
Bas-Tyra
Sadara
WOOD
Silden
Cheam
Malac's Cross
Rillanon
The Kingdom of Roldem
Timons
Durrony's Vale
The Grey Range
The Kingdom Sea
Deep Taunton
The Green Reaches
Mallow Haven
Pointer's Head
The Peaks of Tranquillity
The Empire of Great Kesh

• CHAPTER ONE •

Trap

JAMES CRIED OUT IN PAIN.

He barely managed to pull to the right as the assassin's blade sliced his left side. Any man a scant instant slower in recognizing the danger would now be lying dead on the floor; but James stepped past the out-thrust arm of the killer, wrapping his own arm around the man's neck and drawing his dagger.

Squire James of Krondor, once known as Jimmy the Hand, boy-thief extraordinary, and now personal assistant to Prince Arutha of Krondor, had lived among murderers, thugs and bullies his entire life, and he had faced skilled assassins more times than he cared to recount. The man who had tried to take him down was not as gifted as the members of the deadly

Guild of Assassins, the Nighthawks, but he was no common street thug, either. James knew this struggle would be over in moments, and he was determined not to be the one who ended up lying face down on the cobbles in a sea of his own blood.

The assassin did as James expected, reversing his dagger and slashing backwards into the space James was at that very instant vacating. His left side was hot and sticky, and hurt as badly as any injury he chose to remember, but he knew the wound wasn't life threatening, being no more than a slice across his ribs. It would require plenty of stitches, but it wouldn't kill him. Unless he allowed it to distract him and slow him down.

Ignoring the pain, James let himself fall to the cobbles, then twisted as the assassin lost his balance. He was not willing to let this become a grappling match, as blood loss would quickly give the other man the advantage. Instead he allowed the fellow to fall on top of him. His right elbow struck the stone and pain shot up to his shoulder. Only the frenzy of the fight kept him from losing consciousness. But he held tight to his blade as the assassin attempted to turn and strike.

At the moment when fate decides who lives and who does not, James's blade met the entire weight of the man while the assassin's blade sliced through air.

James felt the man stiffen for a moment, then go limp. He lay motionless for a long, painful minute, refusing to give in to the darkness that was threatening to overwhelm him.

He had been injured enough times in his young life to understand that he was experiencing shock, and that that in itself could kill him. Losing consciousness for any length of time in this particular part of the city was a ticket to certain death. If blood loss didn't do for him, the city watch would find him floating in the bay with empty pockets.

Too many people in this part of Krondor wished to see Squire James dead. Some of their ire was well earned, but some of it was simply a matter of circumstance. The Mockers no longer officially wanted him dead for betraying them, or at least that was how it was told to the rank and file, though in fact his life had been bartered for by the Prince of Krondor in return for saving Arutha's life. Years later, he was still considered to be no longer protected by the Guild of Thieves, but the reality was that he had begun to build a network of agents in the principality.

After a bloody encounter with the Guild of Assassins, and having discovered that the Kingdom's spy network was non-existent, Prince Arutha had charged James with the task of creating an effective intelligence service, so he had started recruiting. Among his first recruits were a number of young Mockers who still regarded him as a friend. But there were still more who would count it a lucky break to be able to brag that they had ended the days of Jimmy the Hand.

Either way, staying in this part of the city for too long was likely to bring an unwelcome end to the night.

James sat up and took a long, deep breath. His side was on fire and his head swam from the pain. He was far enough from the palace that there was a real danger he might not get there before passing out.

He got to his feet slowly, only to have the ground conspire to move beneath them. Making a quick inventory of the people nearby who might do him a good turn, he discovered the list was short. Staggering along, he kept himself upright with a hand on the wall.

Krondor's habitual night fog was thickening, and predators were likely to be shrouded in it, so returning to the palace became doubly problematic.

As a port, the city was oddly situated. There was a growing trade port less than five days' ride south by wagon which would have been an ideal harbour, being south-facing in a wide bay. Even the town of Sarth to the north would have been a better port with some dredging and a man-made breakwater. But the original Prince of Krondor, upon reaching the shore of the Bitter Sea, had declared the promontory upon which the castle was built to be where he'd raise the Kingdom's flag. The standing joke among the palace staff was that Krondor was where it was because the original prince loved the view of the sunsets from that hall.

James had to admit, they were often lovely sunsets.

He realized he was getting giddy and forced his mind to clarity as he stumbled towards his destination. As he moved slowly along, he reviewed how he had managed to find himself in this predicament. Since returning from the north and his very odd adventures involving the mad pirate named Bear, he had been investigating the presence of a rival gang in

Krondor, headed by a mysterious figure known only as the Crawler.

In the last four months life in Krondor had returned as much to normal as it ever did. The prince was busy overseeing the welfare of half a nation, including being the primary spokesman for his brother the king to both the Island Kingdom of Queg and the Free Cities of Natal – the Kingdom's chief trading partners in the west, as well as its chief military threat. Bulk goods from the northern province of Yabon came down the coast to be brokered and sent eastward, while luxury goods from the east and down in the Empire came through on their way to Yabon, the Free Cities, and the Far Coast.

But one thing hadn't returned to normal, and that was criminal activity.

Which was why the Prince of Krondor's personal squire found himself bleeding more than he'd prefer in a side street near the boundary between the Merchants' Quarter and the Poor Quarter of the city. For weeks he had paid every rumour-monger and informant he could trust to provide half-way decent intelligence and had bullied, threatened and bribed any Mocker he could find, in order to try to piece together a picture of what was going on here.

When the Crawler had first appeared on the scene he had been viewed as merely one more interloper, an ambitious upstart who would be quickly destroyed or absorbed by the Upright Man's Mockers. By the time James had left the city to deal with the problem surrounding the theft of the Tear of the Gods – the Ishapian Temple's most revered artefact – he had sensed that something was already different about this gang. There was a relationship between the Crawler and some very evil and bloody magic that was plaguing the principality. He couldn't connect the events of the last few years since uncovering the demon cult in the Jal-Pur desert, the loss of the Tear of the Gods, and other odd occurrences directly to the Crawler and his men, but what James called his 'bump of trouble' told him there was, somehow, a connection, and he intended to discover what it was.

James had undertaken that mission for the prince and the Ishapians a few months previously, and since returning to Krondor he and Jazhara, the prince's advisor on magic, had been poring over reports, searching for those that directly or indirectly referenced the sort of events that might point back to the Crawler and his allies.

A pattern had emerged. Although it centred on Krondor, it extended from Durbin in the west on the coast of Kesh, all the way north to Ylith, southernmost city in Yabon Province. It had taken a lot of work, but the prince had set it as a high priority: the attempted theft of the Tear of the Gods had troubled him deeply. There were few truly sacred things in life, but the Tear was one of them: without it, all the temples in the world would be cut off from the gods for ten years until a new Tear was formed in the mountains to the west. James was one of the few outside the Ishapian Temple even to know that the Tear existed. That knowledge illustrated the level of threat: someone else knew what it was and had tried to seize it for their own use, or to deny it to the Ishapians.

Whether he was architect or agent, James did not know; but that the Crawler played a part in this he did not doubt at all.

He willed himself to take one painful step after another, holding his left arm tightly against his side, using his soaked tunic to staunch the blood flow as much as he could. His mind kept trying to wander, but he forced himself to focus on what he knew so far.

Weeks of enquiry had brought James to a meeting that had a high probability of being between independent smugglers who were avoiding both the Crown's scrutiny and the Mockers' oversight, and an important agent of the Crawler. He had conferred with three of his informants, and then personally ventured out to observe this meeting.

He leaned against the wall and blinked hard, shaking his head, both to clear it and in self-recrimination at his own arrogance.

It had been a trap.

James pushed himself away from the wall and managed to get as far as the corner. He judged the time to be some three hours before dawn: the palace chirurgeon would be less than pleased to be woken in the dead of night to sew up the prince's squire yet again.

Still, thought James as he half-walked, half-staggered through the empty Merchants' Quarter, it wasn't as if the man hadn't done it many times before.

What had struck James about talking with his informants in the basement room of the inn owned by one of the Mockers he trusted most, was that they were truly frightened. A few confrontations between the Upright Man's bashers and agents of the Crawler had produced more dead bashers than expected; moreover, the Crawler had made his intentions clear enough by looting a very special shed near the Royal Customs where items of high value were secreted away until cooperative customs agents came on duty. The contents of that shed were worth a half-year's theft, extortion and robbery to the Mockers, and the Upright Man had put out the word that any man who brought him the identity of the Crawler would be given a lifetime's riches.

The members of the sheriff's constabulary whom James trusted were equally uneasy, as there had been a few run-ins with the Crawler's men over the last few months. Unlike the usual, almost ritual, confrontations with the Mockers – some half-hearted resistance, followed by an every-man-for-himself fleeing of the scene – these fights had been intense and bloody. The sheriff's men were staunch enough lads, but they were not trained soldiers and it appeared that many serving the Crawler had military training. Twice, the sheriff's men had been forced to retreat, calling for reinforcements either from their own ranks or the City Watch, only to find that the Crawler's men had fled by the time they could press home the counter-attack.

Currently, Jonathan Means, the acting sheriff, was James's most important agent in the city. James lobbied the prince almost daily to give Jonathan the position held by his late father, despite the objections of Captain Garruth, leader of the City Watch. The captain was a good man but he wanted the city constabulary absorbed into the Watch, doing away with the office of Sheriff of Krondor; but James had Arutha's ear and had convinced him that a garrison city was not a happy city. He had travelled widely and heard many stories from older Mockers about such cities in Kesh and Queg. James had offered Arutha the alternative solution of integrating the City Watch into Arutha's household guard, the Prince's Own, which would have put Garruth directly under the control of the Knight-Marshall of Krondor, Duke Gardan. The captain of the household guard would be retiring soon, so personal ambition might sway Garruth more than losing authority over the civilian population of Krondor. The presence of three different commands of armed men made no sense to James, and absorbing the Watch into the Prince's Own would create a clear demarcation between civilian and military authority. Besides, James already had tacit control of the sheriff's constabulary as an adjunct to royal intelligence, and he didn't want them being frustrated by well-meaning Watchmen whose charge was ill defined and based on tradition. The Watch defended the city from enemies without and within; the constabulary kept order, while the Prince's Own defended the palace. James wondered at what point someone in authority had thought this was a good idea.

Whilst dwelling on these concerns he had stopped moving

and now found himself leaning against another wall. He couldn't even judge how far he had come. Between his loss of focus and the fog, he wasn't even entirely sure where exactly he was in the Merchants' Quarter. He squinted at a sign above a doorway depicting a bolt of cloth and an oversized needle and finally recognized it as William & Sons Tailors.

He pushed himself away from the wall and took a few steps to the corner. Moving caused him an unexpected moment of clarity. As he rounded a corner giving onto a broad boulevard that would take him straight to the palace, he appreciated the fact that one unintended consequence of this situation had been his ability to return to his old haunts – the sewers and rooftops of the city – almost untroubled. Even though the death mark had been lifted, he had been cautioned to keep clear of the Mockers and their dens, or else there would be no guarantee for his safety. But James, being Jimmy, had ignored that and dared to travel the rooftops or sewers at need, but it had proven cumbersome and at times difficult, for he had often had to lie low while Mockers conducted business between where he found himself and his destination.

During the recent confrontations with the Nighthawks and the quest for the return of the Tear of the Gods, he had done enough damage to the Crawler's men to have earned back some grudging respect from the Upright Man. James was among the most likely to achieve the Upright Man's goal – ridding Krondor of the Crawler – and therefore he was

now a valuable ally to the Thieves' Guild, so the Mocke
had started to look the other way when he went poking around.

James reached a point roughly halfway between his ambush and the palace and stopped for a moment to catch his breath. He clutched his side and felt more blood drenching his shirt beneath the leather tunic he wore. This wound was not going to heal on its own. As loath as he ever was to admit he was wrong, he realized he had underestimated the damage he had sustained.

He heard footfalls, boot heels striking the cobbles coming from somewhere up ahead. The lamps were placed far enough apart that small dark areas lingered between the pools of light, and into one of these he quickly ducked. He had no trust in the Goddess of Luck. Experience had taught him that self-reliance was always his best bet. If there were a god of self-reliance, he'd have been praying to him fervently. He found the irony of that contradiction amusing, or as much as he could be amused, given his current situation.

The footsteps got louder and James struggled to stay focused: there might be a furious minute or so coming up that would decide his fate. He reached across his body and slowly wrapped his right hand around his sword hilt, flexing his fingers and tensing as three figures hove into view.

He was teetering on the brink of collapse when they came walking into a pool of lamplight.

Catching sight of the figure in the shadows drawing a sword, the men slowed and fanned out, each of them also drawing a weapon. Rather than rushing into an attack, they approached slowly. A few yards away from James, the two men on the flanks stopped while the one in the middle said, 'Who passes this night?'

James blinked in confusion for a moment, then pushed himself away from the wall. 'Jonathan?'

The acting sheriff, Jonathan Means, looked incredulous. 'James?'

'I could use a bit of help,' said James.

And then he fell forward, losing consciousness so swiftly that he did not even feel strong arms grab him to stop him striking the cobbles.

• CHAPTER TWO •

Mysteries

JAMES OPENED HIS EYES.

An oval shape hovered above him, and slowly it resolved itself into a face. Dark eyes looked down on him with concern, but there was an amused set to the lips. A woman's voice asked, 'Are you all right?'

James's first impulse was to say something clever, but he couldn't think of anything clever.

The face above him repeated the question.

James smiled and blinked and he finally replied, 'You're so pretty.'

A light laugh was echoed by a deeper masculine one, and someone out of James's sight said, 'I'll send for the prince.'

'It's the drugs,' said another male voice behind James.

He tried to turn and felt agony rip up his left side. A soft hand pushed gently on his shoulder, firmly forcing him back down. A fog seemed to lift from his mind and at last he recognized the face above him. 'Jazhara?'

The Prince of Krondor's magic-advisor smiled. 'Welcome back. We were worried.'

She was a woman of medium height and solid build, though her figure tended to curves and her legs were elegantly tapered. By any measure she was attractive, and she had a no-nonsense attitude that discouraged James's usual tendency to try to disarm ladies with practised flirtation.

The voice behind James said, 'If Sheriff Means hadn't fetched you here quickly, Squire, I think you might finally have left us.'

The disapproving tone brought recognition even though the speaker was still out of James's line of sight. 'Ah, Master Reynolds, again I am in your debt.'

The face of an older man moved into view, hovering over Jazhara's shoulder. It was William, lieutenant of the prince's household guard and son of the magician Pug.

'Help me sit up,' begged James, and Jazhara piled some pillows up behind him so that he could look around the room. As the last effects of the sleeping draught the chirurgeon had given him before sewing him up wore off, pain returned. He winced as he settled into the pillows.

'I've sent for the prince,' said William, walking into view. The young soldier had matured greatly since entering the prince's service and had become James's unofficial partner in crime. James's best friend, Squire Locklear, had been banished to the northern frontier of Yabon as punishment for a transgression involving the wife of an influential man at court. James had thought more than once that women would be the death of Locklear.

William was a different sort, something of a romantic idealist. Taller by half a head than his father Pug, he looked like the icon of the loyal prince's soldier: broad shoulders, resolute expression, brown eyes that gazed unflinchingly upon danger. James often tried to get his goat with a barbed remark, but William would have none of it. He was as stalwart a man as James had ever met, and the former thief actually enjoyed that fact about William.

James sighed as he shifted position, glancing from Jazhara to William. William had obviously been in love with Jazhara before arriving in Krondor, from when they had been students together at Stardock. His attempt to get over her had led to a romance with a local innkeeper's daughter, who had come to grief. He had suffered greatly over Talia's death. In James's judgment Cousin Willy, as he was known to Arutha's family, had succumbed to Talia's charms more because she was crazily in love with him rather than he with her. She had been beautiful, vivacious and a flirt, but once she met Willy, all other boys and men had been forgotten. For most men it would have been difficult to resist. But once Jazhara appeared in the city . . .

James understood the story. He hid it well, but William still cared deeply for Jazhara, or James knew nothing at all.

For his part, James avoided romance. He didn't trust women. More to the point, he didn't trust men. He trusted individuals, and after Chirurgeon Reynolds had departed, it occurred to him that the two remaining in the room were second only to Prince Arutha in earning his trust. Jazhara was new to the court and a Keshian by ancestry, but she had been a staunch ally who had faced deadly danger without flinching. Without her participation in the affair with the pirate Bear and the recovery of the Tear of the Gods, James and William might now both be dead and the hidden enemies behind that artefact's theft might even now be planning to unleash chaos upon every man, woman, and child in the Kingdom.

For a moment the wry thought passed through James's mind that despite their efforts to remain platonic, William and Jazhara were not done with each other. He just hoped, with some apprehension, that things didn't get too awkward or interfere with more pressing concerns.

Now Prince Arutha arrived. He too bore that expression James had come to know so well: the one that was set halfway between concern and wry amusement. 'Almost got yourself killed, again, I see.'

He had changed since James had first met him as a boy, back when he had foiled the Nighthawks' first of many attempts on the prince's life. The youthful whipcord body had broadened a little, and palace life had put a few more pounds on Arutha, but he was still a man of slender frame and as fast an opponent with a sword as James had ever encountered.

'Occupational hazard,' James said, sitting up a little straighter. 'I do recall, Highness, more than one occasion when you were less than prudent when it came to staying out of harm's way.'

With a grimace, Arutha echoed James's last statement. 'Occupational hazard, indeed. However,' he added, 'I find myself bleeding considerably less frequently than you do, James.'

James's grin expanded. 'Well, in fairness, you don't get out as much as you used to. A few days of bed rest and I should be good as new, Highness.'

'We can't afford the time, I'm afraid. I'm sending to the Temple of Sung to fetch in a healing priest. You get one day to sleep off whatever horrible concoction you're forced to drink, then you're back out there the next day.' His expression darkened as he said, 'I do read the reports coming in from Jonathan Means and Captain Garruth, Jimmy. Along with what you've told me, it looks as if we may have something far more sinister going on here in Krondor than a simple struggle for supremacy between rival criminal gangs.'

He turned to leave, then paused. 'You three did well – very well, actually – with that situation up the coast, so I'm inclined to grant you latitude if you think you need it.' Pointing his finger at James, he added, 'As long as you don't get yourself killed.'

James noticed he avoided mentioning the Tear of the Gods directly.

Arutha continued, 'I think it's time to put the three of you back together. Willy, I'll inform Duke Gardan you're on detached duties for a while, so you'd best go do whatever you need to do until James is well enough to wreak havoc in your life. Jazhara, do your best to keep the boys out of trouble, please?'

She couldn't hide her smile as the prince departed for his private apartment.

'Great,' said James, lying back on the pile of pillows. 'A magic healing draught.'

Jazhara smiled. 'I know little about clerical magic: the temples are very guarded about their craft.'

James shifted a little, trying not to groan or wince as he sought a slightly more comfortable position. 'They have their secrets, it's true. Some of the temples are downright hostile if you intrude into what they see as their territory, but I've come across a few clerics who are decent company on a long ride. I think the prince is trying to make a point, as if suffering these injuries isn't enough of a reminder of the danger of some of my choices . . .' his voice rose a little in annoyance, '. . . so I need to choke down a foul concoction to drive the point home.'

'The point being?' asked Jazhara.

'To be more bloody careful in the future,' said James with a wince. He sighed a little dramatically. 'It's not like the prince can't afford the magic. He just wants me to suffer.'

William couldn't help himself from bursting out laughing, which brought a black look from James. 'Some of the temples have magic that will heal you up and leave no scar, even yank you back from the verge of death.' He lowered his voice. 'Some are rumoured to be able to yank you back from the other side of the verge, if the gold is right. There are stories of wealthy men who have made generous contributions to the temple of Sung the Pure, and they have mysteriously returned to health and vigour after a terrible illness or otherwise mortal wounds in battle.'

William smiled, knowing that James was embellishing his tale for dramatic effect. 'Then why,' he asked, feigning ignorance, 'didn't His Highness simply ask a priest to pop over in the first place and wave away your wounds, rather than putting good Chirurgeon Reynolds through such toil?'

'To save gold,' said James with a straight face. 'Our master is a thrifty man, Willy. And he has an evil sense of humour. The healing draught is the most foul-smelling concoction known to man, and this from a fellow who grew up living in the sewers!'

Jazhara put her hand over her mouth and tried not to laugh, but failed. 'I thought you said he was making a point.'

'Well, that too,' replied James.

'Really? You're serious? To save gold?'

'Really,' said James. 'Now, you two go off and let me sleep until the good father arrives. Even with the draught I'll be useless unless I get a good night's sleep.'

William and Jazhara glanced at one another and then made to leave. At the door William turned. 'If you need anything—'

James was already fast asleep.

* * *

'How do you feel this morning?'

'I might be a fair match for a three-day-old kitten, Willy,' said James, his eyes surrounded by dark circles.

Jazhara made a face and William said, 'What?'

'Only James here and the prince call you "Willy".'

'It's the boys,' said James. 'Borric and Erland grew up calling him "Cousin Willy", and Squire Locklear and I picked it up.'

'No one else,' said William. He shrugged as if it was of no importance.

'I find it less than respectful. "Willy" sounds like a kitchen knave's name!' She shook her head slightly. 'You will never hear me call you that.'

James laughed, then winced. He moved his arm on his injured side as if trying to stretch out the muscle.

'Did the healing draught not work as intended?' asked Jazhara.

James stifled a yawn. 'My side is fair, if a bit tender to the touch, but otherwise as good as new. No, it's the other effect of the draught . . . suffice to say I was back and forth to the garderobe many times last night. Sleep came in bits less than an hour long.' Finally the yawn escaped. 'Sorry,' he said, covering his mouth with his hand. 'A good night's sleep and I'll be fine.'

'Then you'll get one tonight,' said a voice from behind. The three turned to see Prince Arutha entering the office from the door that led to the royal family's apartment. He waved them to sit down as he pulled out the chair from behind his own desk. 'I have been reconsidering reports from various sources around the Western Realm, and I think we may have discovered a thing or two . . .' He raised his eyes to James and added, '. . . despite your incapacity. We do manage to muddle along without you.'

James could feel his colour rising while Jazhara and William worked hard to contain their amusement. James was not shy about voicing his opinions on how the business of the Western Realm was conducted, most of which was far outside his area of responsibility or expertise. Yet Arutha indulged him more often than not, and both knew to some degree it was due to the affection in which he held his squire, as well as the fact that James had proved his value well and often. His life had hung in the balance more than once, and he had been an effective agent for the Kingdom since coming to Krondor. Moreover, James possessed a uniquely keen intelligence. Arutha was grooming him for greater responsibility in the future.

The prince was silent for a moment, framing his next remark. James was used to these silences: Arutha was always precise in what he chose to say. Finally the prince said, 'James, I'm releasing you from your office. Find another lad to do those things you leave for other lads to do, anyway. I'm giving up on the notion that you're anyone's idea of a squire. You'll have a new letter of marque tomorrow. You're a knight of the court as of this morning.'

He turned to William. 'I've already told Gardan I'm going to need you away from the garrison, so you'll be holding your rank of lieutenant in the royal household guard, but reporting directly to me only. Is that understood?'

Unable to hide his surprise, William replied, 'Yes, Highness.'

'You three work well together, and I think I'm going to need your full combined attention on this Crawler business. So, beginning tomorrow, your task is to discover this miscreant's identity and bring him to justice. Everything else is secondary. Understood?'

All three of them nodded. 'Good,' said Arutha. 'James, go get some sleep.'

James hesitated, then realizing he was dismissed, stood and said, 'Thank you, Highness.'

'Don't thank me yet, Jimmy,' said Arutha. 'With greater rank comes greater responsibility.' As James turned, Arutha added, 'And more chances to get yourself killed.'

James hesitated for a bare moment, then continued out of the door.

Arutha looked from Jazhara to William and back. 'I don't know what went on between you at Stardock and I prefer to keep it that way. I don't intrude into the lives of my court officers unless their behaviour reflects poorly on my court, or hampers their service. I expect you both to deal with whatever difficulties may lie between you.' He sat back, steepling his fingers. 'James is a young man of prodigious talent, and he has ambition. If I don't keep him on a short leash he'll get himself killed, but too short a leash makes him ineffective; so you two will be my leash when you're gone from the city.'

'Gone, Highness?' asked William.

'It is almost certain, given what we already know, that you three will soon be on your way to Kesh.'

Jazhara nodded. 'Since the night of my arrival, much of what I have seen involving criminal activity in Krondor has involved Keshians.'

'Not all your countrymen in my city can be your great uncle's agents, Jazhara.' Then Arutha revealed one of his rare smiles. 'Though on occasion I'm inclined to think they all may be. Abdur may be the cleverest man I've ever encountered.' He stood up, and they rose a moment after. 'I must return to my other duties. You two keep a close watch on James. He may end up running this nation some day, and I suspect he'll do a masterful job, so don't let him get killed before that. Understood?'

Then without another word, he turned and left them standing in his office.

They exchanged glances and then, silently, departed.

Jazhara waited until they were halfway between the prince's private rooms and the great hall before she said, 'What is it he has heard?'

William shrugged. 'Gossip, no doubt. His Highness keeps a close watch on everything. Rarely is anything undertaken in Krondor or the principality without his being aware of it. Your arrival was anticipated by many, for you are a novelty.' He studied her face, one he knew in every detail from their short-lived romance.

Being a few years older than William, Jazhara had still

been young enough not to understand the difference between their feelings for one another until it was too late. She loved him after a fashion, and had enjoyed the intimacy while it had lasted, but he had been completely overtaken by a deep and abiding love. Their break-up had been bitter and he, being young, had not handled it well.

That had been one of the many reasons why William had decided to leave Stardock and take service with Arutha. The other reasons involved disputes with his father over his role in the Academy. William had what could only be described as a 'magical gift': the ability to hear what animals were thinking. His father had assumed that meant William would take up magic as his calling, but other than the one odd ability, he felt no calling for, nor displayed much talent in, other areas of magic. He wished to be a soldier, a dream of his since childhood, and on several occasions after his fourteenth birthday his mother had had to end a heated exchange between William and Pug.

William stopped and Jazhara turned a half-step later and said, 'What is it?'

William paused, framing his thoughts. 'It doesn't have to be difficult. We've already weathered one . . . adventure,' he said with a pained grin, 'and no doubt we'll face other challenges for the prince. It seems Arutha is putting us in Squire James's – excuse me, Sir James's – charge, and we both know that means a lot more danger and a lot less comfort.'

Jazhara nodded. 'James does attract trouble.'

'Attract? No, he's rather keen to ferret it out,' corrected

William. 'That's why Arutha treasures him so much.' He glanced around. 'James expects to be running this castle some day, and I expect he probably will. But what I mean is, we don't have to make this any more difficult than it already is. That's what I think the prince was hinting at.'

'His Highness doesn't strike me as the type of man to hint, William.'

'Mostly you're right,' said William. He walked on. 'But sometimes he lets the other person puzzle things out for himself—' he inclined his head, '—or herself, because it makes the message much more . . . personal, I guess.'

'So what you're saying is, you're willing to put the past behind us?'

William stopped in mid-stride as if to think about the question, then started walking again. 'I'm never going to forget anything, Jazhara,' he said quietly. 'I'm just not going to let it get in my way, is all.'

'I can accept that,' she said, studying his face.

'What?' he asked after a moment.

'Nothing,' she said with a half-smile. 'It's just . . . you've grown up since Stardock.'

'Being around James ages you . . . rapidly.'

She laughed and they let silence overtake them.

The next morning James, William, and Jazhara were summoned to Prince Arutha's private apartment as he was finishing his morning meal with his wife and children. The twins jumped down from the table and ran over, shouting,

'Uncle Jimmy! Cousin Willy!' and hugged both in turn. They were polite in greeting Jazhara, as she was relatively new to the court and hadn't achieved 'auntie' status just yet. Baby Elena grinned and laughed at the sight of the two 'uncles', then shrieked delightedly.

Princess Anita took a moment to greet both young men, who bowed; and Jazhara, who curtseyed despite wearing trousers instead of a skirt. 'It's good to see you again, boys, and you as well, Jazhara.' She squeezed the young woman's hands. 'You must find time to visit us so that we can get to know each other better.'

Suddenly a yelp of anger and a wailing cry announced that the boys were getting into one of their usual scuffles. Both Arutha and Anita hurried to take care of the baby and herd the boys into the next room.

Jazhara looked at James and saw an almost rapt expression on his face. She smiled.

William said, 'Nothing like my family back in Stardock, is it?'

Jazhara shook her head. 'Nothing like mine either.'

James chuckled. 'This is the only family I've ever known. If I ever do wed, I'm going to try to be as much like them as I can.'

Arutha returned, closing the door behind him. With a rueful smile, he said, 'I wonder sometimes how my father coped with my brother and me when we were young.'

James grinned. 'I believe I've heard parenthood described as "nature's revenge", Highness.'

Arutha laughed briefly, then nodded. 'Well put.' He motioned for them to follow him through another door into his personal study. He sat down behind his desk. 'Very well, where do we start?'

Without hesitation, James answered, 'Kesh. Specifically, Durbin. We don't actually start there, but I'm certain that's where we'll end up.'

'Elucidate.'

William and Jazhara both looked on with interest: they had arrived at a similar conclusion, having discussed it over a shared meal to break their fast before coming to this meeting.

'At every turn we find Keshians involved, Highness,' answered James. 'I've used every contact I have here in Krondor, inside the Mockers and outside, and I've ruled out an attempted takeover both from within the Guild of Thieves – the Upright Man is too smart and has too many loyal thugs at his disposal – or from without. The independent gangs still pay tribute to the Mockers and conduct only the business their small franchises permit.

'What's more,' he continued, 'the Mockers have reached along the coast of the principality up to Sarth and out along the south coast to Land's End. Mostly smuggling . . .' He smiled for a moment and the prince returned the smile. When he and James had first met, with Arutha fleeing Guy du Bas-Tyra's secret police, he had been sheltered by the Mockers and a band of smugglers under the control of a man named Trevor Hull. One unintended consequence of those events had been the eventual wedding of Arutha and his princess, Anita, but the other had been the development of an apparently successful partnership between the Mockers and smugglers that had gone on for years.

'There are moments,' said Arutha, 'when I think making Krondor a tariff-free port would save the Crown more cost than we make arresting smugglers.'

'But where would be the fun in that?' asked James.

With a wave of his hand Arutha indicated James should get back to the point.

James continued, 'We can rule out any sort of encroachment from the east – there is no criminal group of note between here and Salador. There are plenty of criminals between here and there, but they are not organized.'

'So that leaves Kesh,' said Arutha.

'Absolutely. It's possible some group from Queg or the Free Cities might be working for this Crawler, but as we've not found a single Quegan or Free City man so far among the Crawler's crew, logic dictates it's Kesh. And if it's Kesh, that means Durbin.'

'Well, that's the most likely place to start,' said Arutha.

'Not quite yet, Highness. We can't merely take ship to Durbin and wander off the docks asking where we can find the Crawler. We need a convincing story to cover our arrival.'

'What did you have in mind?' asked the prince, his expression revealing anticipation for one of James's more entertaining plans.

• CHAPTER THREE •

Recruitment

MEN SHOUTED.

As the ship came into dock heavy bags of stuffed canvas on ropes, called fenders, were dropped alongside, preventing damaging contact. Still a solid thump and a groan of wood accompanied the last motion of the ship as the dock staff tied her off and the crew prepared to roll out the gangway.

James scampered down the ratlines from the mainmast, then nimbly leapt off the railing to land between two dock workers, startled by this unusual manner for a sailor to depart his ship. He ran to where the gangway was being secured and made a show of lashing down some random rope around a stanchion, then with two steps he was off into the crowd on the pier.

Sir James, newly minted Knight of the Prince's Court in Krondor, had been left behind on the docks of that city. Dodging through the press of sailors, dockhands, prostitutes, thieves, and other assorted miscreants, was one Jimmy the Hand, master thief.

He worked his way through the crowd, watching faces. He moved with purpose as if on his way to a specific destination, but his eyes were constantly seeking out clues as to where he might begin his search. He reached the far end of the docks, where the quay ended and a cluster of hovels occupied the shoreline for several hundred yards, turned and saw a stall where a bored-looking garment-dealer stood.

James knew from his demeanour and position that he was a seller either newly come to the docks or someone who had run foul of whoever allocated locations for merchants – probably a corrupt official in the Governor of Durbin's court – for the only worse location James could imagine would be outside the gates of the city. The man tried not to appear too anxious as James approached, reaching for his belt pouch.

'I travel the sands tomorrow,' said James.

If the merchant was puzzled by one who was obviously a sailor needing caravan garb, he said nothing, but rather broke into a rattling discourse on the high quality of his wares. James ignored him, nodding absently as if listening, but looking for just the right gear to blend into the city. He pulled out a pair of *chalwar*, those loose-fitting, dark-indigo trousers favoured by the desert travellers. These were of good cloth and the merchant said, 'Ah, you have an eye for quality! These are the finest—'

James just continued to nod. He spoke passable Keshian, having dealt with them in Krondor over the years, but his accent clearly placed him as a Kingdom man, so he kept his comments down to grunts and occasional words. Finally he had selected a dark tunic, a matching turban, and a *haik*, a large cloth worn around the body, which was useful in many ways when travelling the desert. In the heat of the day it could be converted to a makeshift tent simply by raising it over the head with a riding crop or some other stick, or even on the hilt of a sword. It was also a blanket when needed, and could save one's life in a sandstorm.

James made a show of haggling, for not to do so would attract attention, and when all was done, he quickly changed his outfit and went back the way he came. He carefully changed his walk from the rolling gait of a sailor to an almost pigeon-toed wide stance, raising his knees like a man used to walking through deep sand. More than one spy had died because the way he moved gave him away. As he followed his previous course in reverse, he saw that the three men he had marked in his first passage were still in place: a barrel-maker who had made no progress on his keg since James had seen him last, an apparently shiftless dockhand who wasn't seeking work or trying to stay out of the mid-morning heat but sat in the sun carefully watching all who walked by, and at the last a prostitute who avoided finding clients.

If Abdur Rachman Memo Hazara-Khan was as clever as

James knew him to be, the head of the Keshian Imperial Secret Police had put these three out to be easily found, while other agents watched who watched them. These other agents were quite a different story: they would be impossible to detect easily, and James knew that anyone he passed by could be working for Keshian Intelligence. He might spend days observing these people before he got a hint of who the true agents were.

Lord Hazara-Khan might be content to leave Durbin's miserable inhabitants to the mercies of the governor's rule, but the city was still a gateway into the Empire, and the head of Kesh's Intelligence Service would wish to know who passed through that gateway, as well as keeping the governor's excesses somewhat in check.

By the time James got to the opposite end of the docks he had spied at least two other agents watching for people such as himself. He knew he would attract attention if he made a third reconnaissance, even in disguise. The docks, like the city square, or other heavily travelled areas of any city, had a rhythm, a flow of people from one place to another, and just breaking that flow would draw notice.

His time was limited, for the sight of a desert man at the docks, while not unusual, was less common than sailors and traders, so he kept walking.

Jazhara and William would be arriving the next day on a diplomatic mission for the prince to the Governor of Durbin. Given the horrors they had encountered so far since the three had been given the mandate to recover the Tear of the

Gods, it seemed a good idea to begin at the top – the governor's palace – and work down as they sought out any magical or demonic influences. Once that charade was accomplished, Arutha had left it up to James to decide how to proceed. Being in Durbin meant they could return to the Kingdom if needs be, or venture into the surrounding countryside should the trail take them outside the city. As Jazhara's people were encamped to the south, her taking a small retinue of guards out of the city by horse or camel would not draw undue attention. James relished the possibilities, and discovered he was also enjoying the responsibilities given to him by the prince. Always without false modesty, and with more than his share of bravado, Jimmy the Hand, now Sir James, Knight of the Court, was finding his rise as addictive as any drug sold in the back alleys. He also discovered that he lacked personal ambition, wishing for no wealth or power for its own sake, but only the opportunity to serve Arutha.

Almost giddy with the realization that he was having the most fun he had experienced in months, he set off to see what Durbin had to offer.

The girl was unusually attractive and a bit unexpected. She was Kingdom-born by appearances, with a fair skin only found along the eastern Kingdom frontier in Great Kesh. The usual tavern dancers in Kesh tended to be buxom and plump, but she was neither. Slender, with a nice roundness in the appropriate places, she had blue eyes and almost black hair. She wore a jade-green costume consisting of a brief top and even briefer bottoms, and a swirl of gauzy veils that floated around her as she danced. She moved slowly to a drum-and-pipe melody played indifferently by two musicians sitting near the tiny stage in the corner. At least this tavern had a stage, James reflected. He had been in a few places where the girl would be kicking over drinks on the bar or knocking food off the table if the customers were too slow in making room for her.

Sipping his second-rate ale, he watched her from the bar as she finished dancing and worked her way through the room, seeking customers for whatever the traffic would bear. Some legendary dancers had accumulated great wealth by being the object of desire of wealthy merchants, at least in Keshian lore. Those stories originated in the great pleasure palaces of the city of Kesh, where nobility and wealthy commoners would mingle and the most beautiful courtesans in the Empire lived in luxury, and where jaded men of immeasurable riches would ignore them too long for dancers they could not have. It was almost poetic, thought James; and almost certainly completely baseless romance. In his experience, women of any type in these places had a price. Still, the tales persisted of dancers who held sway over rich men without ever having to surrender to their desires.

This one, however, was obviously not one of those girls. James thought that had fate been different, she might have aspired to much: she still had a fresh quality, a liveliness that was unusual in this calling. She was flirtatious and smiled a great deal, and James imagined that her Kingdom background would be inviting to those eager to sample more exotic wares, especially with that clear skin and luxuriant hair. After a few years in the taverns, most girls lacked both these traits, concealing the damage of too much drink, smoke, and drugs under a heavy application of cosmetics and hair colouring. They had a listless indifference to their surroundings and daily existence that stood in stark contrast to this vivacious girl. James hoped she understood she was at her peak and needed to take advantage of it while it lasted.

She reached his side and smiled brightly: then her smile turned quizzical. 'If you're a desert man, I'm a tree frog.'

'One doesn't need be from the desert to know how to dress for it,' James answered neutrally.

'A traveller, then,' she observed.

'As are you. Kingdom?'

She nodded. 'By birth.'

'Here?' he asked, with all that question implied.

She laughed. 'Not by choice, I promise you.'

He inclined his head. 'You are unusual.'

'Followed my man here, which was stupid.'

'I think I've heard this tale before,' said James with a rueful smile.

'Self-styled trader. Had a partner in Krondor. Landed here and made all manner of deals, then the partner neglected to send any of the goods promised. I woke up one morning alone, about two months ago, and haven't seen him since. I suspect he's either dead or chatting up another foolish girl in a distant city.'

James nodded. 'How old are you?'

'Twenty winters, and too old to be here.'

He grinned. 'Hardly. You're one of the most attractive dancers I've seen.'

She cocked her head. 'You looking for some private company?'

James considered, then nodded. 'But not quite yet.' As a flicker of disappointment crossed her face, he opened his belt-purse and took out two silver coins. When he slid them across the table she scooped them up and secreted them about her before he could add, 'I may want the night.'

She brightened at that. 'Handsome young man like you, that's not a task.' Then her face took on a reflective look. 'Fact is, you don't strike me as a regular in these sorts of places.'

He laughed. 'I could surprise you.' Standing up, he added, 'Let's say that lodgings where no one is looking are sometimes useful.'

She nodded.

'What's your name?'

She glanced around the room to see who she might approach next, then said, 'They call me "Jade" because I favour green.' She leaned forward and said, 'Truth is, I have only one other costume, and it's also green. My name is Gina.'

He laughed. 'Quegan name.'

'My grandparents, but I was born in Sarth, then lived in Krondor. What's your name?'

He smiled. 'Call me . . . Jim.' He inclined his head. 'I'll be back.'

'I hope you will,' she said, turning and walking away.

He admired the view as she moved away. He most certainly would be back. Spending the night with a beautiful woman was as good a way to hide from Keshian spies as any he could think of, not to mention it took your mind off the harsher aspects of life.

Glancing around the tavern, he picked up his indifferent ale, drained what was left of it, made for the door and vanished into the crowd.

James stretched and yawned as the greying light outside the window heralded the dawn. It was the time of day he loved best if he had managed to get some sleep. It was the time he hated most if he hadn't, because he knew it was unlikely he'd see a bed for another day. This morning he decided he liked it more than not, even though he was tired. His fatigue was of his own devising and was the result of the most pleasant of diversions.

He saw that Gina had kicked off the blanket during the night and lay exposed for his appreciation. She had a remarkable curve to her back and buttocks that made him consider for a moment staying a little longer in bed, but the practical needs of the day trumped more immediate considerations, and he rolled out of bed.

His clothes lay in a jumble on the floor and he dressed quickly. The previous day's efforts had been well spent, and were bearing fruit. Gina had turned out to be quite a bit brighter than one might expect of the average tavern dancer, and had few scruples when it came to spying. She didn't know she was a spy yet, but James would unfold that all in good time.

She would be his first agent in Kesh. Durbin might not be a critical city from the Empire's point of view, but it was of great interest to the Kingdom in the west, given that it was the Empire's only port on the Bitter Sea and more trouble came through Durbin than every other port in the Empire combined.

Gina wasn't educated, but she possessed a street-smart, intuitive ability that could not be taught. James, as Jimmy the Hand, had encountered every woman of low birth you could imagine: thieves, murderers, confidence tricksters, card cheats, whores, shop girls, and drudges. After entering the prince's service, he had encountered women of high birth, and this much he knew: one woman in ten might have survived being abandoned by an idiot lover in Durbin and emerged as nothing worse than a tavern dancer. Most would either have ended up dead, or as slaves, or at best, as whores trapped in one of the innumerable brothels in this pest hole of a city.

James slapped Gina on her bare rump and she said, 'What?' in groggy tones.

'I have a plan,' he said lightly.

She sat up and looked at him through puffy, sleepy eyes.

It occurred to him that she might have the most

beautifully shaped breasts he had encountered, and over the years the number he had seen was impressive. Defying the distraction, he said, 'I think we should go into business.'

She looked at him with a narrow gaze, suddenly suspicious. 'I'm listening.'

'I reckon you are worth a great deal more than an occasional bed warmer for a merchant or trader and that you can do better than being groped nightly for a fistful of coppers.'

She shrugged. She had heard her share of false promises from customers carried away by a night of pleasure. Many a man had left a dancer's bed determined to save her from a life of degradation, only to be barely aware of her name by the middle of the next day. Passion can inflame the imagination as much as it can the flesh.

He laughed. 'I can read your mind.'

'Oh, really?'

'I have no desire to save you.'

She feigned disappointment. 'And I was so hoping for that.'

He made his tone businesslike. 'You're obviously smarter than you let on. Do you know how to listen and not hear?'

She laughed. 'I listen to everything, yet I hear nothing.'

'Good,' he said. 'I would have you listen for me.'

She cocked her head, but said nothing.

'There's a moneylender in the small market by the Low Tide Gate, by the name of Jacob. You will go there and receive a small sum which, should anyone ask, was owed to you by a client who turned out to be honest, if not timely.'

She smiled. 'Then what?'

'Buy something pretty, perhaps a new costume in a colour other than green. Some bangles perhaps, and the smallest dagger you can find, which you should secrete about your person.'

Her eyes narrowed even more. 'And?'

'Start looking around for a spot to open your own tavern.'

'Really?' Her eyebrows shot up. 'What sort of spot?'

'Away from the docks. I wouldn't want your current employer to think you were trying to take away his business.'

She nodded.

'Somewhere on the south side of the boulevard, perhaps halfway between the caravanserai gate and the governor's palace.'

She was silent for a while, then said, 'Some important people tend to congregate in those neighbourhoods, Jim.'

'Indeed,' said James. 'We'll be among them, but nothing too ostentatious. Somewhere among the great gambling halls, brothels and palaces scattered among the nicer establishments, we shall open a modest inn – the sort where those with their fingers on the edge of power are likely to need housing.'

She nodded. 'The sort of place a nobleman's baggage master or a wealthy merchant's agent might lodge – the sort who might let something of note slip with the aid of strong drink and a pretty woman to impress.'

'You're a natural.'

She frowned slightly. 'I have been asked to listen but not hear before, Jim. How dangerous is this going to be?'

'That depends on who you're not hearing while you're listening. Let's say,' he shrugged, 'it could cost you your life.'

She pulled back slightly, and the rising sun played across her face and shoulders. 'You know how to charm a girl, Jim. If my life's at risk, I trust you'll make it worth my while?'

'Your life is at risk every time you bring a man back here. You know that as well as I. You wouldn't be the first girl in Durbin whose customer decided to pay with a blade instead of coin. I'll make you more gold in the next few years than you could see in five lifetimes.'

'And if I refuse?'

'We never had this conversation, and I think you're smart enough not to cause me difficulty.'

She nodded. 'I could betray you.'

'There's an old saying here,' said James. 'There are many holes in the desert, but there is always room for one more.'

'A threat?'

'A consequence.'

'Let me think on it,' she said. 'I have no love for nations nor men of rank, but I do love gold.'

'Smart,' said James with a grin. 'I shall only come by once, in three days' time, and we shall share a drink. If you say nothing to me on this subject, we never had this discussion. If you decide before, go to Jacob the moneylender and tell him your name is Shareena. He will have your gold. Should circumstances warrant, I would enjoy another night here.'

He kissed her quickly on the cheek and left, knowing full well that she would be at the moneylender's stall within a day, two at the most, and to all intents and purposes, James of Krondor, Court Knight to Prince Arutha, had just established his first agent in a Keshian city.

He opened the door, dodged into the early morning crowd and was gone.

Jacob the moneylender looked up at the desert man approaching his stall in the market and for a moment was confused: the desert men never borrowed coin, preferring to barter camels, goats, or whatever they'd looted from travellers. Then as the figure came nearer Jacob recognized his features. He closed his eyes for a brief moment and repressed a groan. His bodyguard, a heavily muscled, black-skinned former pit fighter from the shores of the Overn Deep cast his master a glance. Jacob said, 'I'll need a moment.'

The guard nodded and moved a discreet distance away as James reached the booth.

James raised a hand in greeting.

With his smile frozen in place, Jacob said, 'Jimmy the Hand.'

'Sir James.'

The evil smile remained in place. 'Wave your hands around a little like a desert man, for the gods' mercy, or you'll start drawing attention. A desert man wouldn't be trying to haggle for coin, anyway. Are you trying to get us both killed?'

'Then gesture like I've come to the wrong place and listen carefully, as I won't repeat myself. First, I am here on the prince's business, so from this point forward you'll follow any instruction I give or send you. To know an order is from me, the code will be "Jimmy couldn't come; he's taken a sweetheart." Second, a young woman calling herself Shareena will arrive here within the next couple of days. Account to her ten golden sovereigns or whatever coin of equal worth you choose, but give it to her without question or remark. Should she ask questions, you know nothing. Lastly, she may return to you in days to come, seeking a much larger amount to establish a business enterprise. It's on my behalf, which means it's on Prince Arutha's behalf, so accommodate her as quickly as you can. When you account your expenses to the prince's chamberlain, note these expenses as "payments to James in Durbin on the Crown's behalf", and all will be well. You will be reimbursed within a month with a ten per cent commission added.' He smiled and continued, 'And if you do well in this, in a year or two, you may be allowed to return to Krondor and live.'

'Well, and good, the prince may lift the price on me,' said Jacob, 'but what about the Mockers?'

'I'll see what I can do.'

James turned and left the stall, heading in the direction Jacob had pointed, content in knowing the former tax collector in Krondor – who had fled in disgrace after betraying both his royal commission and his partners in crime in the Mockers – was now his second agent in Kesh. *Who knows*, thought James, *if he serves well, some day he may actually be allowed to return to Krondor*.

Whistling a nameless tune, he dodged through the crowds in the market.

• CHAPTER FOUR •

Arrival

JAMES HID IN THE SHADOWS.

A latticework of rose and amber light cut through the rapidly deepening shadows of Durbin as the sun settled behind the peaks of the Trollhome Mountains. Darkness was advancing rapidly, for the sunset coincided with some heavy marine weather rolling in over the city from the Bitter Sea. James knew there would be a sudden drop in visibility, almost as rapid as someone pulling curtains closed in a room. Soon the Nightwatch would make their rounds, lighting the city's lampposts. Merchants were closing up their shops, shuttering windows and locking doors: the rhythm of the city was changing by the minute.

James hung back in a deep doorway, watching the ship that

was docking on the evening tide. It was a Kingdom freight-hauler, a slow coaster, and on it would be Jazhara and William.

James wore fine garb under his cheap robe. He had luxuriated in a hot bath this morning, having grown tired of the need to look like a rag-picker to blend into the seedier districts of Durbin. On reflection, most districts of this city were seedy. He had poked about in every criminal dive and back alley, even haunting the edges of the slave pens for an afternoon. He had been less intent on finding specific information (though should something material come his way, he would welcome it) than gauging the rhythm of criminal activity in Durbin.

Every city has its own structures, James had learned since joining the prince's service. He hadn't realized that he intuitively understood the criminal organization of Krondor: the Mockers and the independent criminals the Mockers tolerated, as well as the criminals who came to the city to do business with the Mockers. He even understood the relationships between the criminals and some legal enterprises, as well as those members of the city watch who were 'on the arm' – paid a regular stipend to look the other way at key moments. But in dealing with the Crown's needs, James was afforded a perspective from the other side of the ledger, trying to ferret out corrupt officials, to determine which legitimate businesses were fronts for the Mockers' criminal activities. He had quickly learned where to focus his attention and what was worth being concerned about.

Even as a boy he had spent time outside the city, once

for a few weeks dealing with some odd doings down in Land's End, and several times up in Sarth; but here in Durbin, everything moved to an alien rhythm. He was now coming to understand that rhythm. And there was something decidedly strange about it.

Given the power the Crawler had displayed in intruding into long-standing relationships in Krondor, as well as his apparent links to the mad magician Sidi and the pirate Bear, not to mention a mad demon cult in the desert not too far from here, there should have been some evidence of his presence here in Durbin.

There was none.

This troubled James and was on his mind as he watched the gangway being run out from the Kingdom ship. He glanced around and moved to a position alongside the stall nearest the dock, offering him the shortest distance to the gangway without having to cross open ground.

The gangway was secured and Jazhara and William were the first two passengers to disembark. As soon as they were on the docks James was at Jazhara's side, so that suddenly it looked as if three passengers had left the ship. If either Jazhara or William was surprised by his sudden appearance, neither betrayed it, Jazhara simply saying, 'Oh, there you are.'

James said, 'I have rooms for us.'

'Shouldn't we pay a visit to the palace, first?' asked William.

'The governor's not expecting you. A courtesy call is required, but as long as this isn't a diplomatic visit, there's no need to be alacritous.'

James grinned as William smiled and said, '"Alacritous?" You're sounding like a courtier, Sir James.'

'Practising,' said James. He lost his smile. 'Old habits die hard and I've been Jimmy the Hand here for a week now.'

'Any problem with the locals?' asked William.

Jazhara's gaze travelled over the crowd at the docks, looking for any sign that they were being overheard or that magic was being used.

'No, but we'll talk more later.' James glanced around. 'Where's your luggage?'

'And yours,' added Jazhara. 'Offloading it soon, I expect.'

James hurried over to the boss of the dock gang. A quick conversation was followed by a few coins being exchanged, and he returned. 'Come along. I paid the man to have our luggage delivered to our inn.'

'Can you trust him?' William asked.

'Of course not,' said James. 'That's why I paid more to have everything arrive intact, with the promise of more on delivery. A dock gang boss is greedy, not stupid. We appear people of means, so it pays to take what's offered and not incur the ire of someone who may know someone in power. We come and go, but he's there every day.'

William nodded, smiling slightly.

Jazhara said, 'What are we looking for?'

'Let's leave that conversation for a less public place,' James replied.

'We're being watched?'

'Almost certainly. Word will reach the governor within

half an hour that the niece of the very important Lord Hazara-Khan has landed in Durbin with an escort of two minor functionaries—'

'Minor?' interrupted William.

'Minor,' continued James. 'And he will then be wondering what is afoot.' He paused. 'About the same time he'll start worrying if he might perhaps be in some sort of trouble with the Empire or the Kingdom or both, a note from the Lady Jazhara will arrive at his door indicating an unexpected family need has caused her to visit his lovely city, and she would so very much enjoy presenting her compliments in person.' James winked at his companions. 'He'll start worrying again and invite you straightaway, perhaps even for an informal supper tonight.'

They wended their way through the evening crowd, seeing the occasional merchant still trying for that one last sale before calling it a day, walking past open stalls with savoury and pungent aromas as meals were being prepared for those who lived in their stalls, or those who sold food, or those on their way home too busy or unable to cook for themselves. At last they reached a small inn that was crawling with workers. 'Welcome to the Sign of the Jade Monkey,' said James.

Jazhara laughed as she regarded the newly painted sign hanging above the door. It showed a green-furred monkey with its eyes closed, sitting in a cross-legged position with its hands on its knees as if meditating. 'I'm not sure the Jade Monks will find that amusing.'

William chuckled. As he ushered them inside, James said, 'They're a pretty humourless lot, but I doubt one of them will ever see it: they tend to stay in their monastery in the mountains far to the east. Besides, that wasn't really the intent, but a rather happy little accident.' He gestured to a young woman. 'Lady Jazhara and Sir William, may I introduce the proprietor of the Jade Monkey? Gina, also sometimes known as Jade, and she is indeed at times a monkey.'

Gina threw James a dark look for a second, then smiled. 'Welcome. You are our first guests!'

William cast an appraising eye over the beautiful hostess. She was wearing a clinging gown fashioned from green silk and set with pearls. Her jewellery betrayed that she was new to having means, it being both large and gaudy.

James said, 'We'll take a meal upstairs, Gina, given the state of the common room.'

Glancing around, Jazhara and William could see that the carpenters and painters had just gone home, leaving a great deal of work for the next day. James picked up some wood shavings off a nearby table and let them go, watching them for a moment as they drifted to the floor.

'I do prefer my food without sawdust,' said William with a laugh.

James handed Gina a small purse. 'I know our kitchen isn't ready, so have a boy run down to Ahmen's and fetch us back fruit, cheese, bread and wine. Oh, and if Maribeka has any hot sausage left in her stall, on his way back have him grab some of those, please.'

Gina smiled and nodded, hurrying off to do as she had been bid. William watched admiringly as she went, and turned to see Jazhara staring at him with a narrow gaze. 'What?' he asked.

She said nothing but turned towards the stairs leading to the second floor. As she moved off, William threw James a questioning look. 'What?' he repeated. James answered silently with a shake of his hand, communicating that he was not going to get involved in whatever was going on. William could see he was trying mightily to stifle a laugh.

They followed Jazhara upstairs all the way to the top floor. When they arrived on the landing they saw three doors, one on each side and one directly before them, situated down a short hallway. James pointed to the left-hand door. 'Jazhara, that's yours.' Then to the right, 'And Willy, your room.' He opened the door ahead and said, 'And this is mine.'

He led them into a small but well-appointed room. 'Nothing too ostentatious, but nice and clean. We're going to cater to a specific clientele: mid-level functionaries and agents, the sort we'd like to know better.'

'We?' asked Jazhara, removing her shoulder bag and placing it on the floor next to a small table. There were two chairs and a bed, and a modest night stand against the wall under a small window overlooking the street. William took the other chair and James sat on the bed.

The former thief grinned. 'I've purchased the Jade Monkey on the prince's behalf.'

William returned the grin. 'Arutha will be no doubt thrilled with your expending royal funds to purchase an inn in Durbin.'

'I think he will,' said James solemnly. 'At least I hope so.'

'So, a nest of spies?' asked Jazhara, looking a little disapproving.

'Hardly. A convenient place for certain people loyal to Arutha to feel secure when they visit this blight of a city.' He leaned forward. 'Even though I've made this little investment and hired Gina to manage it on my behalf, trust no one who is not in this room.'

They both nodded. Then William asked, 'What is the plan?'

'Rest, wait, and expect an invitation before sundown.'

'What are you going to do?' asked Jazhara.

'The same,' he said, swinging his legs up and lying back on the bed, his arms behind his head. 'I expect that after supper I shall be busy tonight.'

Jazhara and William exchanged glances, then rose and departed. As William turned to pull the door closed behind him he could see that James was already fast asleep.

• CHAPTER FIVE •

Theatrics

THE GONG RANG OUT.

The Master of Ceremony to the Governor of Durbin called out, 'The Lady Jazhara Shala Nema Hazara-Khan, Sir William conDoin, Knight-Lieutenant of the Prince of Krondor's Court, Sir James—' he threw James a quick look at the absence of a surname, then collected himself and continued, '—Knight-Lieutenant of the Prince of Krondor's Court.'

James whispered, 'I think I need to anoint myself with a patronymic.'

'Well, you did somewhat invent yourself, so why not "Jamison"?' William whispered back as they started to walk across the large receiving hall of the Governor of Durbin's palace.

James grinned. 'I rather like that.'

The Governor of Durbin was a heavy-set man with powerful shoulders under a loose-fitting, knee-length robe of fine silk, tastefully trimmed with minimal beadwork. Its one concession to the usual Keshian affection for the ornate was the use of massive pearls as frogs and silver thread in the loops that ran from collar to hem. His sandals were also of fine craftsmanship, though James thought them more utilitarian and less decorative than he would have expected in a Keshian court. The governor stood with his advisors at the far side of the room. James understood the politics here: they had to come to him, and he had the chance to study them as they approached. It was establishing a position of dominance with the niece of one of the most powerful men in the Empire. James conceded silently it was nice theatre, as well.

As they crossed the room, James attempted to identify those who were worthy of notice, deserved attention as dangerous, were merely functionaries, or were purely there for decoration. Like every other human environment, the palace of the governor was a place full of connections, hierarchies, and perquisites. Sometimes titles and offices revealed key elements of those relationships, but more often they didn't. His first visit to Rillanon with Prince Arutha to see his brother King Lyam had taught young Jimmy the Hand, then freshly minted Squire James, that some advisors are listened to more closely than others, that some nobles have more influence and power than others of the same rank.

By the time they reached the governor, who stretched out his hand and took Jazhara's, James had garnered a good idea of who he could ignore, so that he could pay more attention to more important players in whatever game was coming their way.

The governor, Hamet Kazani iben Aashi, bowed just enough to be respectful, and not an inch more; there was no deference towards Jazhara. 'Welcome, Lady Jazhara. I am a great admirer of your uncle. How is Lord Hazara-Khan?'

'Well, last I heard, Governor, and I have no reason to expect otherwise.'

James resisted the urge to smile at her use of his office title, rather than the general honorific of 'my lord', for Governor Aashi was a commoner who had elevated himself by wit, skill, and a ruthless, murderous ambition. James had read every document on him before leaving Krondor, and had concluded the governor was effectively the King of Durbin, given how little imperial oversight came from the City of Kesh. He was a man who was jealous of his position and all the trappings of his office. And therein, James thought, might lie his vulnerability.

The governor said, 'Would you please present to us your companions?'

Again, James resisted an urge to laugh. Jazhara might be someone to whom he must show deference, but the two minor knights from the Kingdom were men he could pretend to ignore; or at least, he could ignore the introduction just made by his own Master of Ceremony.

Jazhara said, 'Sir William conDoin—'

At the mention of William's surname, the governor's attention shifted, and James realized that this had thrown him off balance, just a little. 'ConDoin' meant a relative of the King of the Isles, and no matter how distant that relationship was, the bearer would always be a man of some importance.

'—And Sir James Jamison.'

The governor threw James a perfunctory smile and nod, then turned his attention back to Jazhara and William.

James listened as the governor chatted with William, pausing occasionally to smile in James's general direction, but James could tell he had already consigned James to a 'not very important' role in his mind. Perhaps the lady had two lovers, or a lover and his friend, but whatever that relationship might be, the governor was concentrating on people he considered important, those who might be used to his advantage, or who might somehow pose a threat. To be inconspicuous was exactly what James wanted. He would endeavour to fade into the background as best he could through the evening, so that by dawn tomorrow, if all went well, the governor wouldn't even be able to remember what he looked like.

Now, the governor took Jazhara by the arm and steered her towards a large table that had been surrounded by couches, in the Quegan manner. James thought this a bit odd, but as Queg was merely a week's sailing to the north, he presumed the governor had visited, liked their dining style, and installed it in his own court.

A regal-looking woman stood before them and the governor made introductions. 'My dear, this is the Lady Jazhara, Sir William and—' he glanced over his shoulder a little, '—and Sir James, from Krondor.' To his guests he said, 'My wife, Lady Shandra.'

James and William bowed slightly, while Jazhara extended her hand and the Lady Shandra took it. 'We are honoured to have you in our home,' she said.

She had been a stunning beauty in her youth, James decided, for despite the grey in her hair and having gained a little weight, she was still a striking figure. She had dark eyes and full lips; her face was slightly lined, but she used powder and rouges to good advantage. But beneath the striking exterior, there was something else. The subtle way her husband's behaviour had changed told James that while the governor might rule the city of Durbin and the surrounding environs, Lady Shandra ruled this house. And something else was causing James's 'bump of trouble' to itch. For no reason he could name, he marked this woman as dangerous.

A servant escorted them to their places, and James reclined on one of the couches. After finding a comfortable way to lie and accept titbits from passing trays, he found himself next to a young traveller from somewhere in the heart of Kesh, a dark-skinned man who looked more like a warrior than the merchant he claimed to be. James assumed he was one of the governor's agents and guarded his conversation accordingly.

The dinner proved tedious: as James had anticipated, the companion on his left attempted to gain information about why the lovely Lady Jazhara was in Durbin – not the most direct route to see her family, should she be travelling into the Jal-Pur – and what could James tell him about the young knight travelling with her: how closely was he related to the royal family? The attempts, being clumsy, were easily evaded. James stuck to the prepared story: Jazhara was travelling this way because of some minor family business in the city, and because her family was in residence at an oasis closer to Durbin than Shamata, and because rumours of raiders in the eastern Jal-Pur made this route more prudent. As for the good-looking young knight-lieutenant, he was a very distant cousin to the prince and king, bearing a name but little rank, wealth or influence. However, the Lady Jazhara and he had formed a very close relationship.

When the meal was over and the three of them were safely back at the Jade Monkey, in Jazhara's room, James looked at her and said, 'First, did you sense any magic?'

'Something,' she said, looking uneasy. 'I couldn't put my finger on it, as it was unknown to me. It was either a long way away, or close and subtle – I'm not sure which.'

'Assume close and subtle, to be on the safe side,' said James. He was silent for a moment, then added, 'Could it have been demonic?'

Jazhara was thoughtful for a few seconds. 'Perhaps. I have little experience with demons or their magic. The one encounter under that inn in Krondor was the only time, and while I watched the priest banish the demon . . .' She shrugged. 'It's a bit like listening to someone speak in a language you can't quite understand.'

James shrugged. 'I have a bit more experience, I'm sorry to say. Demons have been showing up from time to time since I first took service with Arutha.'

William had heard some of these tales. He asked, 'Anything we need to watch for?'

James shook his head. 'I don't know. After that run-in in Krondor I asked a bit here and there from some of the clerics inclined to talk about the subject. The Order of the Shield of the Weak at the Temple of Dala have collected quite a bit of demon-lore. All I know is, the ones I've run afoul of are big and nasty. That one we saw in Krondor was a tiny thing compared to the monster that showed up at Sarth when I was travelling north with the prince.' He paused as if remembering. 'Something one of the prelates said back then . . . I may be suffering from faulty recall, but I seem to remember that some demons are from another plane.'

William nodded. 'What they call the lower hells.'

'Whatever that is,' said James. 'But others are made, conjured out of dead body parts and the like.'

Jazhara shuddered.

'And some are invisible,' added James. 'I must poke around. You two need to look like illicit young lovers stealing away for an impromptu assignation disapproved of by both your families.' He grinned. 'Or at least by your nations.'

As Jazhara's family was a powerful one in Kesh and William was related to the royal house by adoption, it wasn't far from the truth. 'I'll have Gina fetch you up some wine.' James stood up. 'I'm going back to my room to take a nap. I need to be out tonight and have to be seen here and there a little tomorrow.' He reached for the door. 'Try to look convincing.'

William blushed as the door closed and Jazhara tried not to laugh. At last she said, 'What have you told him?'

'About us? Nothing, really, but Jimmy has his ways of finding things out, and if there was a rumour about us in Stardock, he'll have heard it by now, have no doubt.'

'We should talk,' said Jazhara.

William's brow furrowed. 'I thought we had.'

She smiled. 'So did I.' She paused. 'I didn't realize for a long time how much I'd hurt you, William.'

It was obvious he was uncomfortable with the conversation. But he returned her gaze and nodded.

She sighed, moved in towards him and put her arms around his waist. Laying her cheek against his chest, she said, 'I know you think I toyed with you, but that wasn't the truth.'

'What was the truth, then?' he asked quietly.

She was silent for a long moment, then said, 'I did love you, William, in my way. I was older, true, but I was also young and without much experience.' When she looked up at him he saw a slight sheen of moisture in her eyes. 'I did love you.'

He felt his chest tighten. 'I know I was only a boy, or so you thought, but I . . .'

'What?'

He gathered her close. 'I knew other girls after you left.' Slightly bitterly he added, 'I'm Pug's son. Any girl at Stardock . . . you know?'

'I know.'

He sighed. 'But there was no joy in that. The simple truth is, I love you, have always loved you and will always love you.'

She tightened her grip around his waist. 'I loved that boy,' she whispered. 'And when I finally found you again, you'd become a man.'

Suddenly she rose up and kissed him, deeply and long.

William awoke to the sound of James clearing his throat. Jazhara's head was on his chest: they were both under the blankets of the narrow bed. Looking towards the door, he saw James leaning in with a bemused smile. 'Ah . . . when you're ready. My room.' He closed the door.

William looked at Jazhara for a moment, then both began to laugh. He pulled her close and kissed her and she responded for a moment, then pushed him away. 'James is waiting.'

'Let him wait.'

But Jazhara rolled away from him. In doing so, she almost fell out of bed, which resulted in more laughter. 'Later, we have ample time later.'

He watched her as she dressed, admiring every curve of her body. 'We have a lifetime.'

She halted for a moment. 'Really?'

William sat up and reached for his trousers. 'Since I left Stardock I've had a couple of . . . encounters. And my affections for Talia were real, but there's only you, Jazhara. There has never been anyone else.'

She pulled her tunic over her head. Then she came and knelt before him. Cupping his cheek in her hand, she said, 'Last night was . . . amazing.'

'But . . .?' He tensed, as if ready to pull away.

'There is no "but", William. I loved you as a boy. I think now, as a man, you are more than I expected.'

He studied her face, then said, 'When you're ready, I will speak to the prince.'

Her eyes widened. 'To Prince Arutha? About what?'

'We're both in service. We need his permission to wed.'

'Wed!' she exclaimed. 'Are you daft?'

He grinned. 'If I am, it's you who make me so.' He let her go and grabbed his tunic, then paused. 'Or are you saying no?'

'I'm not saying yes,' she returned. She sat on the bed next to him, pulling on her boots. 'I'm not saying no, either.'

He laughed. 'Five years it's taken for me to break through that barrier.' He stood and gathered the rest of his gear, then looked at her as she pulled on her second boot. 'You might as well relent. I will have my way in this.'

She couldn't help but laugh. 'Well, if that's the way it is going to be, you can stand before both our families and explain how this is all going to work out with everyone's blessing.'

He was too happy to consider just how difficult that was

likely to be. 'Seriously, you are the only woman I have ever loved. The only woman I ever *will* love.'

'And I love you, William, son of Pug.'

He opened the door. 'I can hear my father now: "I wanted you to *be* a magician, not to marry one."'

She laughed, stepped across the hall, knocked on James's door and went in.

James grinned at them. 'I can't say you underplayed your part as illicit lovers.'

Before they could speak, he went on, 'I don't care. What you do is your own business, and my only advice is, don't let your feelings get in the way of our work for the prince. Though I hope this removes that annoying awkwardness between you.' He glanced from face to face, then sighed. 'Or doesn't make it worse.'

'We're getting married,' William said.

'I haven't said yes!'

James held up his hand. 'What did I say about not caring?' He shrugged. 'Well, good luck, you two.' Then he turned solemn. 'I've spent a long night following up on some leads and I've come to a conclusion.'

'What?' asked William.

'There is no Crawler.'

Jazhara stared at James. 'I don't follow.'

'If I were a stranger in Krondor, poking around the way I have been, one of two things would have happened by now.' He held up one finger. 'Either I would have found evidence of who was in charge of the different gangs and who they worked for, or,' he held up a second finger, 'I'd be dead, because someone would have tumbled to the fact I was poking around before I noticed.' With a grin he added, 'The first is rather more likely than the second.'

'So, what have you found?' asked William, sitting on the bed beside James as Jazhara pulled up the single chair.

'Nothing. There's nothing going on in Durbin to suggest there's any sort of organization of criminals here, like the Mockers, or the Ragged Brotherhood in the City of Kesh.'

William laughed. 'Perhaps it's because everyone in Durbin is a criminal?'

Jazhara threw him a dark look.

James said, 'Well, Willy, as much as we love to malign this fair city, that may not be far from the truth. The Captains of the Coast are pirates, but all carry marques from the governor, making them "merchant privateers", whatever that means. And the Kingdom's navy is content to ignore them as long as they don't trouble Kingdom-flagged ships. Let them annoy the Quegans and the merchants of the Free Cities, and look the other way at the rare transgression against the Kingdom, and we have peace on the Bitter Sea, or at least what passes for it.

'And there are the merchants' societies, all of them secret, and some guilds, and all of them have people working in the governor's customs house and the like, but nothing on enough of a scale to cause the status quo of business in Durbin to be upset. So if there's a dominant criminal gang worth the name in this city, I've not found it.'

'I don't understand,' said Jazhara. 'Everything we've uncovered said there was Keshian complicity in the Crawler's activities.'

William said, 'You don't suppose your uncle . . .?'

She looked embarrassed. 'My uncle is a very powerful man. He's the de facto ambassador to Prince Arutha's court in the west, but the rumours about him being the head of imperial intelligence . . .'

'Which does not exist,' said William and James simultaneously.

Jazhara said, 'What?'

'Old joke in the prince's palace,' said William.

'Very old joke,' said James. 'Your uncle is undoubtedly the master of the Empire's spy network, but he's so gifted we can't even prove that the network even exists.' He stood up and looked at William. 'However, everything we do know about Keshian intelligence tells us they wouldn't be that artless. No, Lord Hazara-Khan has nothing to do with the Crawler; I'd stake my life on it.'

He moved to the door and opened it for them, indicating their meeting was at an end. 'You two, run off and shop or eat in a public place or do whatever it is you'd expect a pair of runaway lovers to do. You have two more days to linger in Durbin before the governor becomes suspicious about your tale about travelling to see your family, Jazhara.' He grinned. 'I'd tell you to try to be convincing, but I guess we're long past that.' As the pair reached the door, he added, 'You might spend some time thinking up what you need to tell your families and the prince.' With a grimace he added, 'It's at times like this I'm rather pleased I don't have a family.'

They left and he threw himself across the bed. The last remark made him think that the only person he ever needed to convince of anything was Prince Arutha, which at times was probably worse than having an angry father.

He rolled over on his back, kicked off his boots, and was asleep in minutes.

• CHAPTER SIX •

Ambush

JAMES JUMPED FROM THE ROOF.

The sound of boot heels on tiles echoed behind as he struck the cobbles below, rolled and came up running. He'd have a nasty bruise on his shoulder to show for this night's foray into the seediest part of town, but it was better than a broken ankle with three murderous thugs only seconds behind him.

He gained a few more seconds as they hesitated at the roof's edge. A nasty cracking sound and a howl of pain told James one of the three had indeed jumped and broken an ankle or leg. The others had most likely grabbed the eaves, hung from them, then dropped.

James looked for a place to go to ground, as he had no desire to lead these three back to the Jade Monkey.

He found what he was looking for in some low, overhanging eaves above a stack of timber. He stepped on the wood carefully, trying not to lose his balance or make a sound, reached up and leapt. Grabbing the eaves, he pulled himself over, and moved back so that he could not be seen from the street.

James had become frustrated at not being able to clearly identify anyone in the city who might be part of any criminal organization, so he had decided it was time to cause a fuss. Playing the part of a thief newly come to Durbin, he feigned drunkenness at several of the taverns near the docks, dropping hints along the way that he was in possession of something of value and needed the services of what was known in the criminal parlance as a 'fence', a dealer in stolen property.

One burly dockworker followed him from one inn to two others and finally, when James appeared to be close to insensible from drink, told him he knew of a fellow, and would bring him if James stayed put. James nodded, instantly recognizing this for what it was, an attempt to abduct him and force him to tell the bullyboy and his lads where the valuables were stashed.

He recognized an ambush; he just didn't know what he faced. He waited in the tavern, having scouted it thoroughly before entering, and thus knew there were at least three escape routes, depending on how he was attacked. He was adept at sipping a little ale and spilling a lot when no one was looking, and no one was likely to notice a spreading pool of ale at his feet under the stale straw that covered the floor.

After less than an hour, the man had returned and gestured for James to follow him outside for the introduction to the fence. Two steps outside and he knew exactly what the situation was: three men closing up on him, one following him out of the inn, one from each side. So he leapt atop a parked cart and onto the roof of the building across the street and took off, not looking to see if he was being followed, expecting that he would be. And indeed, moments later he had heard grunts of exertion and curses behind him, and knew he was off on a chase he knew well.

Lying flat on the rooftop, he waited to see if his two remaining pursuers were smart enough to work out he had lost them, and backtrack. James hoped so, for he needed to follow them, and have them lead him back to whoever employed them. If they gave up the hunt somewhere else in the city, all this exertion would have been for naught.

Then a flickering shadow on the rooftop across the street caught his eye. He waited, not moving, to see what was there. He almost willed the gloom to reveal what it masked while he kept track of his pursuers by ear. He could hear their footfalls echoing into the distance and when he could no longer hear them, he waited to hear them return.

A boy's lifetime of being a thief had taught James patience far beyond his years; if need be, he could lie motionless for hours, ignoring the plague of distractions that a less practised man would find maddening: an itch to scratch, the desire to shift position, hunger and even thirst. On more than one occasion his life had depended on that skill.

Time dragged on but James was convinced there was someone hidden in the blackness across from him, almost certainly just on the other side of the roof's peak, sheltered against the remote possibility that an observer might catch sight of him. That gave James pause, and worse, a dread certainty that he knew who was mere yards from his hiding place. And if he was right, he prayed to Ruthia the Goddess of Luck he had not been seen pulling himself up on the roof moments before he had spied that movement. Then he thought if he had been seen, most likely he would be dead.

After another long five minutes, James heard the sound of footfalls approaching, lightly, slowly, cautiously. His two would-be captors were indeed retracing their steps, trying to ascertain where he might have given them the slip. He heard whispers, though he couldn't make out the words. Their tone was frustrated and urgent. Someone wanted the drunken, loud-mouthed thief and wanted him badly.

As they neared, James saw a hint of movement on the opposite roof, then abruptly a figure came over the peak of the roof, half slid down the eaves, and with an effortless, fluid move, pulled a short bow off his back. In an almost inhuman act of speed and precision, two arrows were loosed and the two men chasing James lay dead on the cobbles.

James tried even harder to blend into the roof tiles and fought back the urge to either run or slip backwards. Any movement would surely instantly end his existence.

Time dragged and then suddenly the archer was gone. James didn't move. He closed his eyes for a second, then looked again. It was fully five more minutes before he dared move enough to glance over the eaves into the street. Below lay the two men, pools of blood spreading around them, each with an arrow through the throat, which had denied them even the opportunity to cry out.

James rolled over and looked up at a blank sky, the stars hidden by the marine clouds that came in from the Bitter Sea. He let out a slow breath and gathered his wits.

The archer's identity was unknown to him, but he was a Nighthawk, a member of the Brotherhood of Assassins, a group with which James was all too familiar. He and Prince Arutha had seen the destruction of their hideout in an abandoned fortress miles to the south.

He waited for another five minutes, thinking how like rats they were. If you didn't get them all in their nest, they were out in the sewers or on the rooftops, breeding.

'Damn,' James whispered to himself. At last he slowly got to his feet, looking around for any possible attack. When none came, he lowered himself from the eaves and dropped to the stones, quickly vanishing into the night.

• CHAPTER SEVEN •

Departure

JAMES YAWNED.

William and Jazhara glanced around the common room of the Jade Monkey, which was quiet at the moment, as the workers were out securing materials. One table had been erected in the corner and three chairs provided, and Gina had had a newly hired porter fetch a meal from a nearby establishment.

'You need sleep,' said Jazhara.

'I'll get some, just not any time soon.' James's gaze travelled between the faces of his two dinner companions. 'You ready to leave, Willy?'

William nodded. 'I've found us escorts, and Jazhara's family is camped at an oasis only three days away.'

James considered. 'Who did you find?'

'Izmalis,' said Jazhara.

James closed his eyes for a moment. 'They're a little too close to being Nighthawks for my liking.'

Jazhara said, 'They work for my uncle.'

'Of course they do.' His face took on a calculating expression. 'How many?'

'A dozen, all hard-nosed veterans, from what I can judge,' said William. 'We're going to move as quickly as we can, but stop after a day's ride to see if we're being followed. If we are, we'll continue on to Jazhara's family and assume no one who means us ill will blunder into a camp of over a hundred desert fighters. And if no one follows us, we'll send the Izmalis on without us, double back and be waiting at that wadi a half-day's ride to the southwest.'

James nodded. He knew it well, having passed through it on his way to the Valley of Lost Men and the ancient fortress known as the Tomb of the Hopeless. 'If I need you, I'll send a message. You'll know it's me and not some trap because the messenger will tell you "James has lost his way", and if he says anything else, kill him and flee. I will already be captive or dead.'

'What are you going to do?' asked Jazhara.

'I've got this bad feeling that we're dealing with the same crew we tangled with in Krondor when we were trying to get back the Tear of the Gods, the same lot who tried to grab that wrecker Kendaric, to get him to raise the Ishapian ship.'

'Bear's crew?' asked William.

'Bear's boss, or bosses. There was a lot about that entire fiasco that really doesn't make sense, and I'm not sure that magician who helped you was really who he said he was.' Then he added, 'There was something about that fellow . . .'

James shook his head. 'It doesn't matter, because what I know is that there were Nighthawks and demons involved then, and there were Nighthawks and demons involved down at the Tomb of the Hopeless, and if there are Nighthawks here, then we can probably expect a demon or two.'

James stood up. 'I'm going to visit a couple of temples and see if I can find someone who knows more about demons than I do – which should probably mean anyone I talk with – and see if there's some means by which we can find out if there is demonic magic at play. Then I'm going to see if I can do something impossibly stupid.'

'Go looking for the Nighthawks?' asked William.

'First try, Willy.'

Jazhara said, 'William, would you give James and me a moment alone, please?'

William glanced at her for the briefest moment and then nodded, and left the inn to wait outside. When he was gone, Jazhara said, 'William will be anxious to return.'

James raised a quizzical eyebrow. 'He's young and doesn't want to be left out of the struggle. But why the sudden concern, Jazhara? Willy's been through more than men twice his age.'

She smiled. 'I know. But that encounter on the bluffs with

Bear, when William was filled with the power of Kahooli . . .' She shrugged. 'He doesn't speak of it.'

'Willy spent just about his entire life on an island full of magic-users. He was used to seeing miraculous things by the time he was ten years old.' He saw that she was unconvinced. 'What is this really about, Jazhara?'

'He . . .' She sighed. 'We were lovers some years ago on Stardock. It didn't end well. I do not know what this . . . new thing between us is, but I know my feelings have changed. He was a wonderful boy then; now he's a man. A man who's seen much and braved much and . . . I think he has lived up to his promise. I just do not wish to see that cut short because of his unwillingness to be cautious.'

James nodded. 'I'll do what I can, but you must remember, first he is a sworn servant of the prince, and second he is a soldier. Danger is part of the bargain.' Then he grinned. 'Still, Willy's not as foolhardy as Locky, who you'll meet one of these days.' His grin broadened. 'And if he hasn't changed much, he will be very pleased to make your acquaintance, though I'm sure that will seriously annoy Willy.'

She laughed.

'What?'

'Willy. That name.'

James returned the laugh. 'As I said, it's a habit Locky and I picked up from the twins, Borric and Erland. We're Uncle Jimmy and Uncle Locky, and William is Cousin Willy. It just sort of stuck. Some of the soldiers do call him Will, but mostly it's William.'

'Will?' She considered that for a moment, then said, 'I'll continue to call him William.'

James laughed. 'Whatever makes you happy, Jazhara.'

He walked with her outside and called, 'Willy?'

'James?'

James lowered his voice. 'I want to amend something. If no message is forthcoming, don't come looking for me. Come back here and see if I left anything with Gina and then, either way, return to the prince. If I vanish, that will tell us this Crawler is far more dangerous than we thought. The prince will need to know about the Nighthawks as well.'

William frowned. 'I thought that went without saying.'

James smiled. 'I just wanted to make sure. I didn't want you attempting some ill-conceived search.'

William glanced at Jazhara, then nodded. 'I see.' He sighed. 'I'll do as you ask, James.'

'Good,' said James. He looked around. 'Where are your Izmalis?'

'At the east gate next to the caravanserai. We have horses and supplies there waiting for us.'

'Then be off!'

As they left, James let out a long sigh. He had no problem with the two of them falling into bed together, but he had serious reservations about them falling in love.

Returning to the Jade Monkey, he wondered at this improbable thing called love. He was certain that he'd only seen it once in his life, and that was between Prince Arutha and Princess Anita, and he judged this wonderful mystery was as rare an occurrence as those two people. It might be nice to feel that way about someone, some day, he thought as he caught sight of Gina coming out of her little office at the back of the inn, but until that day, he'd be content with taking his pleasure where he found it.

Gina noticed him watching her and smiled. He returned the smile and considered for a brief moment following up on the implied invitation. Then he realized he had too much work ahead of him, and headed upstairs to plan his next foray into the city that night.

• CHAPTER EIGHT •

Instruction

THE MONK LEANED FORWARD.

'The thing about demons,' Brother Eli said, then paused to take another draught from a large tankard of ale, 'is they're sneaky bastards.'

After Jazhara and William had departed, James had spent the afternoon at several of the temples in Durbin. By Krondor's standards they were modest at best, hovels at worst, but their followers were as devoted as those in the largest temples in Rillanon. To James's amusement and amazement, the man he sought out was made manifest in this rotund monk of Banath – Ban-ath, as he was called in Kesh, as opposed to Ba-nath as he was known in the Kingdom – patron god of thieves, liars, gamblers, as well as a few more socially appreciated trades. He was also the god of risk takers and those inclined to rely more on their skills and cunning than the random whim of Ruthia, Goddess of Luck.

In striking up a conversation at the shrine, James discovered Brother Eli to be an affable fellow, well disposed to indulge James's curiosity so long as it was over a tankard of ale. Several tankards, if the progress of his story-telling was any indication.

'What do you mean, sneaky?' asked James. 'I've had a few run-ins with demons and they were a little too large, nasty and loud to be called sneaky.'

'Ah,' said the portly monk. He pointed a meaty finger at the former thief. 'I took you to be one who formerly trod the dodgy path, young sir.' He fixed James with a squint which caused the two bushy red eyebrows above his pale blue eyes to wiggle like caterpillars. His almost-bald pate was surrounded by a ginger fringe, and apparently the hot sun of Kesh's north shore had given him a perpetually sunburned scalp. 'Come to better circumstances, by the look of you,' he finished.

'What makes you say that?'

'Only the foolish – and you do not appear to be such a one – and those devoid of luck – and again you do not strike me as such – and those who are in the wrong place run afoul of demons.' With a barking laugh, he added, 'As we've already disposed of ill luck as a reason, you had to want to be in the wrong place.'

James laughed, remembering the three times he had run

into demons, at a distant abbey, in an abandoned fortress full of killers, and in a basement. 'I can promise you, brother, I had no desire to be where I found myself at that time.'

'Why don't I believe you?'

'Given your calling, one can wonder,' said James.

'It's true,' said the monk, indicating that his tankard was empty. As Jimmy signalled to Gina to fetch another, Brother Eli continued, 'We who serve the Trickster as well as we can, well, let's say our flock is not one predisposed to trust.'

James found the man's candour refreshing. The high-ranking prelates of Ban-ath in Krondor were a sanctimonious lot who avowed that their god was as essential to the natural order of things as any other god or goddess. James took no issue with matters of faith. He had prayed to the god of thieves on more than one occasion when his life hung in the balance, and even made votive offerings after surviving a few lucky escapes, but he took that as a duty more than devotion.

Gina appeared with a fresh tankard. 'It's a necessary thing, don't you see, to accept all the whims of nature, and our god is as much a part of the natural order as any other. Those who are able take from those who are less able. It's the way things are.'

'Demons,' said James, getting him back on topic. 'Sneaky bastards?'

'Yes,' said the now red-cheeked cleric, after draining off the new tankard. 'See, I had this brother who heard the calling to Sung, the Pure, and he became a demon hunter.

Didn't see him much for years, then we both ended up here.'

James nodded.

'We caught up on old times, some family lore, and over the years when he was in Durbin from time to time he'd stay with me at my hovel behind the shrine. Not much in Durbin for those pure of heart, don't you see? Not a lot of support for that temple. Anyway, he'd tell me this or that about demons and their doings and the like.'

'Sneaky?'

'Ah, yes,' said Brother Eli, waving Gina to bring him yet another tankard without bothering to ask James. 'See, for reasons no one seems to understand, some demons want to be here, doing whatever mischief they can. Lots of theories as to why, you see, but no one really knows. The kind you spoke of – big, loud, angry – those are the conjured ones, the ones yanked out of the lower hell and brought here against their will to do the summoner's bidding. Lots of stories about it all coming to a bloody end.' He lowered his voice. 'Nasty business, that. But some demons – the sneaky ones – they find a way here without being summoned. Now the lore says that each time a demon appears without being summoned and is unconfined, heaven sends an angel to hunt it down. If they come to blows, as soon as one is vanquished the other returns to heaven or hell as the case may be. Doesn't matter who wins; they just cancel each other out, so to speak.'

'Interesting,' said James.

'But that's not what you were asking about, is it?'

James shook his head.

'See, those you were talking about, those are the corporeal demons, from another realm, and they need magic to survive here, either their own or the summoner's. Some can rampage around a bit and cause a fair amount of havoc without it before they vanish back to their realm or an angel arrives, but there's another kind.'

'Another kind?' Now James was very interested.

'You hear of possession?'

James thought back to his encounter at Haldon Head with the false priest, Father Rowland, and nodded. 'I have seen something like that, but it was . . .' James paused, then explained that the false priest of Sung had been an agent of a dark force, and that he had in turn controlled the towns-people, electing to dispose of those not easily controlled, and that with his death, his control vanished.

'Ah, that's a different kind of proposition,' said Eli. 'See, there are dark agencies that grant a man a power, and mind control is one of the darkest, but that's not what I'm talking about. No, I'm talking demonic possession.'

Gina brought the next ale over and removed the empty tankard, and Eli watched as she walked away. In a lowered tone he said, 'Quite the shape on that one, right?'

James looked at him questioningly.

'We're not a celibate order, lad.' Eli pointed from Gina to James. 'You two?'

James sighed. 'Demonic possession?'

'Good,' said Eli. 'I mean, good about you two, not demonic possession. Ah, yes. See, there are these demon spirits. They enter our realm without a body, either by some agency we don't know or because someone fouled up a summoning spell and got one of the spirit demons instead of one of the big and smelly corporeal ones. So this spirit is casting around, don't you see, looking for a place to stay, and tries to take over some hapless person, the weaker the better.'

'That sounds horrible,' said James.

'It is, lad. It takes an unusually powerful mind to resist such a creature. Even magic is no protection if it's not the right sort. It's why all the temples look down on demon-summoners. They're like babies playing with fire in a thatched hut.' He lowered his voice as if not wanting to be overheard. 'But even more vile is the fact that there are those who willingly offer themselves as hosts.'

'Really?'

'There are many tales and some well-documented events chronicled by the different temples, telling of such "deals", as they're known.'

James gave a humourless chuckle. As a member of the Mockers he knew many deals were unhappy accommodations that yielded little joy.

'I know. I know,' said Eli, 'but some people are driven by a thirst for power or a need for revenge or some other dark desire that makes them think such a deal is worthwhile. The thing is, the poor soul is pushed aside, as it were, witness to all the horrors the demon inflicts on others, helpless to do naught but watch. And if the deal is not struck cleanly, often they lose their ability to ever regain control.'

Thinking about what he'd seen so far, James asked, 'Why would anyone serve demons?'

'That's a question no one of reasonable mind can understand, lad. Many stories tell of promised riches and power, a place at the demon's right hand when they gain whatever power they seek, but history teaches us demons are all liars and oath-breakers. Unless they're bound by ritual and runes, confined in a ritual circle, they'll take free rein.'

'How do you . . . fight them?'

Pushing himself away from the table, Brother Eli stood up. 'I need to get back to the shrine. Thank you for the hospitality.'

'How do you fight them?' James repeated.

'Oh, well, there's the usual. They can't cross salt.'

'Salt?'

'It's a symbol of purity,' said the monk. 'You can confine them in a circle of salt, or erect a barrier of salt, and they can't pass.'

'Can't they just blow or sweep it away?'

'You'd think so, but no, they can't.'

James sighed. 'OK, so that sounds temporary.'

'It is. But it may buy you time to fetch a priest to banish the demon back to hell and free the host.'

'What else?'

'They don't like the touch of iron. They can abide a brief, glancing touch, but if you hold it to their skin a few moments, it starts to burn them.' He turned, then looked back at James and added, 'Oh, you can always kill the host, which banishes the demon back to hell.'

'Sounds like a bad solution for the host.'

'Aye, lad, but it's better than having your soul enslaved or your mind destroyed. A demon can live a very long time, and to be stuck in its head for centuries is a sure path to the most painful madness I can imagine.'

'Is there anyone here in Durbin who can banish a demon?'

'Not with any certainty,' said the monk. 'Most of us in the city might give it a bash, but you really need one of the higher-ranking prelates from the big temples, perhaps of Kahooli, Sung, or Dala. The followers of Lims-Kragma don't abide demons well either.'

James nodded his thanks and watched the monk leave as night began to fall. Instead of finding answers, he was overwhelmed with more questions.

• CHAPTER NINE •

Discovery

JAMES HURRIED ALONG THE ROOFTOPS.

Since his encounter with the Nighthawk, he had donned a different disguise and spent two days poking around the darker alleys and seedier inns of the city, trying to puzzle out what had happened to him during his last chase. Someone wanted to catch the new thief in the city, but the Nighthawks, or someone employing the Nighthawks, didn't. This presented James with a dilemma: he could certainly appreciate why someone would want to question a drunken thief who might have something of value in his possession, but he couldn't begin to speculate why someone would not want that drunken thief caught, let alone send a Nighthawk to shadow him and protect him.

For it had finally dawned on James that for the Nighthawk to have killed his pursuers, the black-clad assassin had to know where James was and where he was likely to go to ground. With chilling clarity, James realized that the Nighthawk knew he was on the roof opposite and had waited there to kill the two men chasing James, and for whatever reason, he did not want James dead, for if he had, James would have been dead.

As a boy, luck and circumstance had saved James once before in confronting a Nighthawk on the rooftops. His other encounters had also proved that his luck was near endless. He had survived his last run-in only because he was being saved as a sacrifice to conjure a demon, or he would never have regained consciousness in that cell below the old keep in the Valley of Lost Men.

James had found no rational motive for why the Nighthawk was trying to keep him out of the clutches of those thieves, and the absence of any logic in this was driving him to distraction. He had faced a lot of challenges in his young life, but this one was perhaps the most exasperating.

James reached his destination and lay down, then moved forward to peer over the edge. He had presumed that if no one in the city was clearly in the network of the Crawler or obviously a Nighthawk, they had to be coming into the city from some location beyond Durbin's walls. He had spent two nights in other locations, and tonight his choice of observation point was a pair of streets where the first road up from the easternmost end of the harbour intersected with the street leading to the eastern city gate. This should have been his first choice, he thought, as this intersection gave anyone here quick access to the docks, the city gates, or straight to the governor's palace.

Smuggling into Durbin was almost comical: the imperial customs service was so corrupt you had to pay a huge bribe to get a position with it. But the norm was to look the other way when someone was smuggling contraband *out* of the city, not *in*. To choose the cover of darkness to come into the city suggested an unusual reason – and in Durbin that would have to be something extremely nefarious.

James had noticed a few things during the course of the last two nights that had led him to pick this location. The city watch had a predictable circuit, but they avoided this corner of the city, it appeared. And there was just something a little too quiet about this part of Durbin.

Even in the dead of night, there is an atmosphere and rhythm to every quarter. In Krondor, James would have noticed any such disruption of the norm, but Durbin was new to him and it would take longer than the time he had to acclimatize himself to the city. He'd have to trust his instincts.

Besides, if nothing came of tonight's search, there was always tomorrow night.

He waited, trying hard to stay alert despite the lulling silence, which was punctuated occasionally by some distant sound from another quarter of the city. There was a stillness in the air that was common to the coast of the Bitter Sea as the hot inland winds pushed out against the onshore sea breezes. James knew that as the sun rose in the morning and the desert furnace was reignited, a hot wind blew at this time of the year, forcing approaching sea captains to take a long tack from the northeast, then jibe due south into the harbour mouth, where they would be towed into the docks by eight-man tugs.

James forced himself to look down empty streets, pushing aside a tendency to drift off. More than one Mocker had been found dead on a rooftop, his throat cut while he dozed, and young Jimmy the Hand had let others' mistakes be his teacher.

After more than an hour of waiting, he heard an unexpected sound, the light squeaking of a horse's leathers. He chanced a glimpse over the eaves and saw four riders in black moving slowly towards the gate. He quickly measured their direction and saw they came from the vicinity of the governor's palace and were heading for the eastern gate. The hooves of their mounts were muffled with leather covers so the sound of iron shoes on cobbles would not announce their passage, but the occasional snort of a horse or the sound of leather upon leather was impossible to mask. At any other time than the dead of night, the sounds would have gone unnoticed.

The riders might have been Nighthawks, or merely travellers in black, but James suspected the former was more likely than the latter.

But where were they bound? Had they been trailing Willy and Jazhara, they would have left two days ago, and through the southern gate, not the eastern. James fought down the impulse to race after them, knowing that he wouldn't get far on foot and that by the time he secured a horse they'd be long gone.

Still, there was nothing to prevent him from heading back from where they appeared and seeing if something useful could be uncovered.

He moved silently along the rooftops until a street prevented him from going any further, then dropped to the cobbles below. He could make out no signs of recent passage in the gloom. This was not a heavily used street. He assumed those travelling in stealth would take the shortest route to the gate, so he followed a straight line, glancing at every intersection in both directions for anything that might look like a point of origin – a large warehouse, a stable, a road leading to an estate. But all he saw were modest businesses, many with homes above for the owner and family, and a couple of small inns – nothing that could house one horse, let alone four with riders.

He reached the end of the street and found himself looking directly at a gate that led into what he assumed was the stabling yard of the governor's palace. Looking around, he realized there were several large estates nearby, any one of which could have housed the four riders.

He had narrowed down the possibilities for their point of origin, but he still wasn't sure. As he took a moment to decide in which of the two possible directions to explore, he caught a whiff of a familiar odour and smiled. You could muffle a horse's hooves, wrap rags around bridles and ride as silently as possible, but you couldn't train a horse where to leave manure. James didn't even have to inspect it to know it was fresh.

The four riders came from the governor's palace.

James glanced around to see if anyone might have caught sight of him, though if anyone did, all they'd see would be a man of unremarkable height and build wearing a head covering and dark clothing.

He took off at good speed, not quite a run, but fast enough that should anyone need to follow him, he'd hear them, dodge into the first side street he encountered, and waited. When he was certain no one was following, he made his way quickly back to the Jade Monkey.

• CHAPTER TEN •

Hunting

JAMES HID.

Deep in the shadows opposite the governor's palace he watched the gate through which he suspected the Nighthawks had ridden three nights before. He had dispatched a messenger to the agreed-upon location where Jazhara and William waited.

He had spent the last three days snooping as best he could in a half-dozen guises: merchant, traveller, sailor, and mercenary warrior. He had collected a fair wardrobe that he now thought of as his costumes, and with Gina's help had quickly come to master just what a little make-up could do for a man. A couple of touches with a brush could make his eyes look deeper sunk, or his cheeks hollow, or give him the sunburned look of a desert man.

He was finding her to be an unexpected treasury of useful information. Slowly a pattern of how business was conducted in Durbin was emerging and he was now convinced that the reason he never could discover the criminal organization in Durbin controlled by the Crawler was because one simply did not exist.

The Crawler and his ring of thieves and smugglers were a convenient fiction devised by someone associated with the Nighthawks doing business right under the governor's nose – unless he was part of the plot – and it was designed to divert suspicion away from . . .

That was where James came up dry. He knew Jazhara's uncle already had agents in Krondor. So the Crawler and his mythical gang were not one of his enterprises.

And there was Nighthawk involvement, which meant . . .

James had no idea what that meant.

So he was out hunting for information – any shred of a suggestion of a hint that might put him on the tracks of whoever had created this fictitious Crawler and his criminal empire.

His first encounter with the Nighthawks had been to foil an attempt on Prince Arutha's life, soon after the Riftwar when Arutha had returned to Krondor after his brother had been crowned king. That was the event that brought Jimmy the Hand once more to Arutha's attention and began the rise of a boy thief to the position of a minor noble in the prince's court.

As best as could be pieced together about that attempt,

the Nighthawks had served some dark agency that had sought to kill Arutha as the fulfilment of a portent that was to signal a major uprising of the Brotherhood of the Dark Path – the dark elves – as they launched an invasion of the Kingdom. It wasn't until the rogue dark elf chieftain Gorath had come south to warn the prince of a second attempt at whatever was hidden in Sethanon – the cursed city – that James had begun to understand the magnitude of what was in play.

His subsequent encounters with the Nighthawks, his privileged status with the prince, and his general curiosity about things he should not be poking around in, all brought him a keen awareness that whenever the Nighthawks appeared, they were only part of something bigger and more dangerous than he fully understood.

One day he might have a better sense of what was afoot, but for the moment he was only concerned as to why Nighthawks seemed to have established a base somewhere within the premises of the Governor of Durbin's palace.

Time passed slowly and the balance of the night was spent in frustration. As dawn neared, James decided nothing of note would be forthcoming.

He was less than fifty yards away when he heard the sound of the gate he had been watching opening, and had to duck into the sheltering darkness of a deep doorway. Moments later four horsemen came riding by, the muffled hooves of their mounts making a dull clacking sound as they sped past, turning right at the next intersection so that James knew they were making for the southern gate. Years of street living had equipped James with what he had come to term his aforementioned 'bump of trouble', and now it was nagging at him. He knew somehow this pre-dawn departure had something to do with the message he had sent to William and Jazhara.

Suddenly he felt himself a fool.

While he had been watching the Nighthawks, they had been watching him. If they wanted him dead, he would be dead.

He decided it would be best to consult with Jazhara and William before planning his next move. As he went quickly through the dark streets he felt something he rarely experienced: uncertainty.

For most of his young life, James had displayed a self-confidence that often bordered on the arrogant, a certainty of ability that made many of his decisions seem precipitous and capricious, but underneath this brash surface was an almost inhuman ability to calculate probabilities. He was hardly aware of it, as it was something that had come naturally to him all his life, and had he the temperament he would have made a stunning gambler. But sitting at a game table for hours was not in James's nature. He had, however, met few whom he thought might best him at any card game or any other game of chance.

That innate ability had served him while in Arutha's service, for he either knew what was at risk and what was the reward, or he knew where to find the information he needed to make those judgements. His 'bump of trouble' often kept him from rash decisions, but at every turn James felt as if he was making progress, somehow gaining new information, new insights, new understandings, or proof of his correct judgements.

This time, nothing.

James missed his best friend, Squire Locklear. One of Locky's more useful traits was his ability to silently listen while James rattled off suppositions, observations, or wild theories. More important, Locky had the knack for redirecting James to one point he had made in his long ramble, one thing said that would turn out to be the key to the entire subject under discussion.

William and Jazhara were each brilliant in their own way, but neither had that particular knack of conversation Locky had. Still, once they returned, James was determined to sit the two of them down in his room and just recount everything, to see if they could spot something he had missed.

He wended his way through some dark alleys, cutting across empty boulevards. He chose a long, looping route back to the Jade Monkey, not wishing to lead anyone there if he had been followed.

A hundred yards away from the inn he ducked into a shallow store-front just shadowy enough to hide him. After slowly counting to a thousand, he knew he was not being followed. He dodged out of the doorway and across the street, then into a small space between buildings, up on to the roof of the building that backed up against his little inn. He had inspected this area for several reasons, security being foremost, but also against the possibility that he might need more land. His inn lacked a stabling yard, so he had to have someone fetch horses and camels to a stable some distance away, which currently was an inconvenience, but in the future might cost him business.

One advantage he had gained in inspecting the entire neighbourhood was discovering a back way into the Monkey, over the rooftop of the house behind. Standing on the roof gave him quick access to the window of the room he had chosen for himself. To facilitate such an entrance, he had secreted a sturdy wooden crate from which he could easily reach the window above.

He stepped lightly on the crate, avoiding making any noise that would disturb the woodcarver who slept below, and reached up to grab the bottom of the window ledge. He pulled himself up to eye level, glanced in, and saw movement.

Lowering himself again, he waited to see if his movements had been noticed. Whoever was in his room must have been watching the door against his return and ignoring the window. Jimmy controlled his breathing as he squatted on the box beneath the window and wondered how many other would-be attackers were in the Jade Monkey. Were he planning this, he'd have a few at the bar or tables drinking quietly who would let him go past to his room, then close in behind him if the assailant in the room failed.

And what of William and Jazhara? Had they already returned to walk into this mess? James knew the Izmali guards would be dismissed as soon as they entered the city, or would return to Jazhara's family camp from their hiding place. So they would be on their own.

James slowly uncoiled himself and took a quiet step away from the window, shifting his weight as carefully as he could to avoid the roof tiles betraying his presence.

Then the window behind him exploded in shards and splinters and a black-clad assassin hurled himself through the opening to seize James around the waist. The tiles cracked beneath the impact and James and the assassin rolled down the roof until they came to the eaves. James felt a shock run up his left arm from elbow to shoulder as he slammed it against the roof to halt his roll. His attacker continued to roll for another second as James got his dagger out of his belt and struck. He felt the blade hit ribs and cut along them, and the man grunted in pain and surprise. James remembered too vividly just how painful that would be, but he also knew it was not an incapacitating blow.

Instead of pulling back his blade for another strike, he kept it pressed hard against the man's side. No matter how well trained he might be, any fighter who was not overcome by rage and the rush of combat would react to pain, if only for a moment. The instinct was always to pull away from it.

James heard metal on tile. As he was lying across the assassin's right arm, he surmised the man was pulling a blade from across his body with his left arm. James dragged the point of his own blade across the man's chest, down towards his stomach, and heard the man groan as he struggled to get into position to strike.

When the assassin pulled back to reach his knife, James reversed his own blade and struck upwards, under the man's chin, driving his dagger deep into the throat. There was a gurgling sound and a fountain of blood struck James in the face, blinding him. A moment later the attacker went limp.

The entire struggle had lasted less than a minute.

James lay panting from exertion and pain. His left arm throbbed so badly, he wondered if he had cracked a bone stopping their roll down the roof. He shook his head and forced himself to focus.

He pulled loose the dagger, wiped it clean on the man's black tunic, and took a moment to examine his attacker. He would not linger, for he knew there was a good chance those in the inn had heard the noise on the roof and might be hurrying up the stairs or moving out into the street to cut him off.

Ignoring the blood pooling everywhere, he knelt next to the dead man, opened his shirt and found no Nighthawk pendant.

James sat back, catching his wits and his breath. He shouldn't have been surprised the man wasn't a real Nighthawk; had he been, it would probably be James lying there in a pool of his own blood. He did a quick examination of the man and found no purse, nothing in the pockets, no other clue as to who he was and who had sent him.

The crash through the window must have alerted someone, so James decided to get away and ponder all this later. His left arm and shoulder throbbed: he would be sporting an assortment of bruises for a week.

He awkwardly levered himself down the eaves and dropped to the stones, and as he did so he heard pounding on the door of his room above. He glanced around to make sure the way was clear, then vanished into the night.

• CHAPTER ELEVEN •

Snare

WILLIAM POUNDED ON THE DOOR.

He and Jazhara had arrived an hour before sunset, had been told by Gina that James had been away for the last few days, and after eating, had retired to their respective rooms: despite their rekindled love for each other, both were bone-tired from the journey and elected for a good night's sleep. Having heard the noise from James's room, they had come to investigate.

'James!' William shouted as he pushed hard against the locked door.

Jazhara said, 'Stand aside,' and as William did so, she closed her eyes and incanted a spell. The wood around the lock-plate above the door-handle cracked and splintered, and the plate sounded as if it had been hit by a sledgehammer. 'Try it now,' she said.

William pushed. The wood around the fractured lock-plate resisted for a moment, then crumbled inward. He shoved with his shoulder, then drew his sword and stepped inside.

The room was empty, looking as it had the last time they had been there, save for the shattered window. William hurried over and peered out, seeing a dark shape lying on the rooftop of the building behind the inn. He was about to tell Jazhara what he had seen when he heard a muffled cry.

A large man had grabbed her from behind, clamping a meaty hand over her mouth and dragging her out of the room.

'Jazhara!' William spun to aid the magician. As he turned the corner into the hall, a heavily gauntleted glove slammed into his cheek, nearly cracking it, causing him to bounce off the splintered door jamb back into the room. He staggered, tripping over a fallen chair, as his attacker came into the room, a lethal-looking dirk at the ready.

William grabbed the side of the broken window to halt his backwards progress then stabbed out with his sword. He had no hope of impaling the man, but it did cause his attacker to back away.

William righted himself and crouched. He was a soldier, and while brawling was occasionally an off-duty pastime, he was conditioned to the discipline of being part of a unit of men. His opponent, on the other hand, was much more versed in one-on-one combat, as a thug, brawler, assassin, or whatever he was. The man measured the distance separating them, feinted to his left, then charged.

William tried to recover and stepped back a half-step, avoiding the bull rush and dirk point, but the assassin drove his shoulder into William's stomach, carrying them both to the window and then through it, with William's left arm wrapped around his attacker's neck. Wood splinters flew as the two heavy bodies smashed through the already-broken window, and William hung on for dear life. In such circumstances his sword was useless; but the other man's dagger was an impaling weapon designed for in-close fighting. One thrust and William would be dead or mortally wounded.

With a grunt of exertion, William attempted to keep his opponent off-balance as they flew through the air before crashing into the roof tiles of the building behind the inn. A terrible cracking sound rang through the night as they slammed into the roof hard enough to crash through both the tiles and the wooden sheeting beneath.

William felt shock go through his entire body from the impact and fought to stay conscious. Beneath him, the assassin went limp. A broken neck hadn't been William's intent, but this wasn't a fencing match with rules: this was life and death.

William found himself partially held in place by the splintered wood below the tiles. He moved gingerly, trying to find a way to get out without causing more damage to his back and buttocks, even though he was frantic about what was happening to Jazhara. And at any moment another assailant might be coming though that window.

He forced himself up and out of the depression, ignoring the howls of fear and outrage coming from the inhabitants of the room below.

He rolled over and got to his knees, catching his breath as he examined the dead man. The assassin was not a Nighthawk, for he did not wear the traditional garb, nor carry the pendant. He did, though, have a small coin purse in which William found twenty golden Keshian imperials, about the value of fifty Kingdom sovereigns, a handsome sum for a street tough. William thought it was probably the price of tonight's attack.

Whoever had orchestrated this abduction didn't want Jazhara dead, or they wouldn't have hauled her away, but rather would have dispatched her on the spot. The man who had grabbed her from behind could, just as easily and rather more safely, have cut her throat.

William rose, looking down on the burly man with the bent neck. And whoever hired this motherless dog didn't care if he killed William or was killed by William. His sole duty was to distract him long enough for Jazhara to be carried off.

William caught his breath, picked up his sword and looked around. The shouting from the room below had ceased after he had stopped moving on the rooftop. He saw the box under the window James had placed there to facilitate entry and made it from one roof to the next. Crawling back through the window got him additional splinters and cuts, but he ignored them.

He hurried through James's room, down the stairs, and into the common room. Gina lay on the floor. William knelt, but was relieved to discover she was merely unconscious. From the bump he felt on the back of her head, as long as she didn't have a broken skull she'd be fine in a few days. He looked around the room and saw another form lying on the floor, a customer who had been bludgeoned into unconsciousness. William inspected him and found him alive, if barely. He moved both prone figures to a relatively safe location behind the bar and then stood up and surveyed the damage.

The common room was mostly intact, so the thugs who had come to attack them had entered quickly and quietly. Jazhara and William had been in their rooms, and William had still been in the hope of a late-night return by Sir James. Otherwise he would have been fighting that thug in his smallclothes rather than a heavy-duty tunic and trousers. Given the number of splinters he could feel in his back and sides, he was glad he had not undressed for bed.

Jazhara had been less fortunate, for she was wearing the simple singlet she slept in. Not only was she without her usual belt-dagger, she did not have her belt-pouch which contained her magical trinkets, potions, and powders. Even so, her innate magic ability was prodigious, so those who had captured her must have possessed some means of counteracting that.

Which meant she was the target, as he had suspected.

He stood motionless, looking down at the unconscious

barmaid and the guest, uncertain what to do next. Going to the Durbin authorities would probably be next to useless: as the cousin-by-adoption to the royal house of the Kingdom of the Isles, he would receive all manner of reassurances and promises, but he knew the governor and his court would be far more likely to look for someone to blame so that they could present someone's head on a pike to Lord Hazara-Khan while explaining how a member of his family had been abducted. It might prove smart politics, but would contribute nothing towards finding and retrieving her safely.

William was frustrated. He had no idea what to do next. His normal sense of responsibility and duty was overlain by his rediscovered passion for Jazhara. He now knew she was the woman he was fated to love for the rest of his life. His budding romance with Talia the innkeeper's daughter had taught him that love came in many forms, and that there were many worthy people deserving of that affection, but Jazhara was that special person who made his life complete. He had seen such a love between his mother and father who, despite being born on different worlds to profoundly different cultures, managed to bridge the gulf between them with a passion that still abided.

He would not lose that. For he knew that if he did, he would never find its like again.

He took a deep breath and one more time looked around the room. *What would Jimmy do?* he wondered.

• CHAPTER TWELVE •

Improvisation

JAMES WINCED.

'Stop twitching. This is hard enough as it is,' said Brother Eli.

James had arrived at the shrine of Ban-ath at sunrise, and behind it had found the monk asleep in his tiny shack. Now James lay face down on the monk's disreputable bed. He vowed that his next votive offering to the God of Thieves would be bedding and a fresh blanket for the monk. Eli dug into him again with a needle and fished out another nasty wooden splinter. 'There,' he said triumphantly. 'That's the last of them.'

James started to rise but the monk's beefy hand pushed him back down. 'Let me put some unguent on those so they don't fester. Some of those splinters went fairly deep, lad.'

The monk fetched out a jar from under a table piled high with books and scrolls, and unscrewed its metal lid. The stench that struck James was enough to make him jerk back. 'What is that?'

'It's a concoction whose composition was taught to me by Brother Regis at the abbey outside Shamata. Mostly tallow with a healthy dose of sulphur and a bit of willowbark ground fine, some crushed moonflower seeds, and a bit of henbane to stop the pain.'

'It stinks like a sewer, and I know sewers.'

'As I well know, Jimmy the Hand.' He started applying the ointment, dabbing it over each puncture.

'Jimmy the Hand?'

Eli laughed. 'A young noble from Krondor by the name of James comes skulking around asking about dark subjects, and you don't think my curiosity is piqued? I appreciated the ale, lad, but also was wondering what you were doing here, so I had one of my acolytes watching you at the Jade Monkey. Every night, he says, this young court knight from Krondor comes skulking out of his window, drops down from the roof, and off he goes. Then he runs across rooftops, jumping from there to here and back. He lies down and watches, waiting, for what?

'Then two nights back my boy says four riders come back all dressed in black with hooves muffled and gear tied in rags, and all stealthy-like they ride out of the city, and our young lord from Krondor is watching them like a hawk.' Eli slapped James lightly on the shoulder. 'Put on your tunic, lad. The stink will fade.'

'Good, because right now you can smell me coming a block away.' James sat up and put on his tunic. Moving his shoulders, he said, 'Thank you, Brother Eli. The wounds do feel better.'

The monk put away the jar and continued, 'So I'm thinking to myself, those must be assassins, those four riders. And while Durbin may be the most miserable hive of miscreants in the Empire, we are still the doorway to the Bitter Sea, and traders and travellers and sailors come through every day from all parts of the Western Realm. And you know what they bring?'

James shook his head with a slight smile.

'Stories,' answered the monk. 'They bring tales of a boy-thief who saved the Prince of Krondor from the Nighthawks and was taken into his court. Oh, not all at once, you know. A bit here and a bit there, and not a few Mockers have wandered into my shrine over the years. You piece this bit and that bit together and after a while you have a story, don't you?'

He sat down next to James and grinned. 'Besides, if my master has a favourite, it has to be you, young sir.'

'I'd like to think so,' said James. 'But he can be a difficult patron at times.'

'Isn't that the truth?' said Eli. 'The Trickster has his place in the scheme of things, you know. He's a bit of a rogue and most of those visiting my shrine are ne'er-do-wells embarking on a caper, or those who fear thieves and mountebanks; but in the end, they're all asking for his protection.'

James chuckled. 'The bookie who gets his cut if he wins or loses, right?'

'Something like that.' The monk's tone turned serious. 'There are things coming, my young friend. Perhaps not in my lifetime, perhaps not even in yours, but some day things are coming that will threaten the very existence of life as we know it, and when that day arrives the best any of us can hope for is to be ready to confront the thing we fear the most.'

'Which is?'

'Ourselves, young Lord James.'

James smiled. 'Not a lord . . . yet,' he added with a wry twist. 'One day perhaps, but for the moment it's Sir James, or if you like, Jimmy.'

Putting his hand on James's shoulder, Eli said, 'Well, Jimmy, your reputation precedes you. So if all you need is my help in removing a few splinters, you've got it. If you have secrets to keep, that is your right. But if I can be of further service . . .' He raised an eyebrow. 'You were asking a lot of questions about demons the other day.'

'I have my reasons,' replied James.

'I have no doubt,' said Brother Eli. 'I have learned years ago that my master is among the most difficult of gods to serve, as he's an aspect of life that most people would not care to consider most of the time. The random nature of Ban-ath's acts tends to unnerve those who think the universe flows in an orderly, natural pattern.

'But I have learned since my acolyte days that the universe is far more complicated than any of us will ever understand and the roles of our gods are not necessarily what we think them to be at times. Demons are by nature . . . well, they're not natural,' he said with a shrug. 'Or at least not in this realm. They come from somewhere else and don't belong here.'

'Then why do they want to be here?' asked James.

'You mean the ones that aren't summoned?'

James nodded.

'No one knows, or at least no one who's written anything on the subject. I did a little poking around after our last conversation and I have a friend who's a prior at the Temple of Dala. They're among the most keen demon-hunters in the world: their Order of the Shield of the Weak specializes in ridding this world of demons.' He rose and reached over to his cluttered shelf and pulled down a small book. It was leather-bound and ancient. 'He lent me this.'

'What is it?' asked James.

'A little tome penned by a monk named Auric of Tyr-Sog, copied several times by the order of Dala. This is the prior's personal copy which I shall shortly return to him.'

'Anything interesting in it?'

'Two things, really. One is an attempt at a taxonomy of demons, which isn't half bad once you learn to ignore the terrible writing and love of flowery description. The second is a reference to an ancient Keshian text reputedly in the library in Queg, the title of which loosely translates as *The*

Large Great Book of Demons.' He held out his hands. 'I think it means it's both a large book and great with details.'

'Next time I'm in Queg I'll give it a glance,' said James, wincing slightly as he moved his left arm. 'Don't suppose you have anything for a banged-up shoulder, do you?'

'Not among my skills, sorry to say.'

'Don't think anything's broken, but I thumped that arm and almost dislocated my shoulder.'

'Let me look.' He gently reached over and touched James's shoulder. Then he gripped it hard, one hand on the front, the other on the back of the joint, and twisted. There was a loud pop, followed almost instantly by James gasping in pain. 'Nothing almost, lad. That was a partial dislocation, and I've set a few. Many of our master's followers have a nasty habit of falling off roofs or walls and the like.'

James rubbed his sore shoulder and forced himself back to the subject in hand. 'The book?'

'Yes, it details a bit more of what I was telling you, about the different types of demons.' The monk seemed almost enthusiastic. 'There are three general types, as I said: the big physical monsters that get summoned, a few of whom even have their own magic, and those that seize the bodies of humans and take them over. And there are those that can shape change, and look like humans.'

'Shape change?'

'A few. From what I've been told that's a very difficult magic. Usually, they cast a glamour, to fool the eye.'

James shook his head. 'Seems to me that the spell that

would do that would be big enough for a good magician to detect.'

'I would expect so, too, but then we're not talking human magic here, are we?'

James sat back. 'Tell me more about those spirit demons that take over humans.'

'Well, let's see,' said the monk, thumbing through the small book. 'It says here, once they take over a human they become very difficult to kill. Seems it's partly to do with the magic and partly that they don't care how much damage the human takes because it's not their body. If the host dies, they flee.'

'Flee? Where?'

'Some speculation on that subject, but most sources suggest they return to the lower hells. They have to have a second living host nearby to leave the first one and move to another; again, this is mostly speculation.'

James said, 'So, difficult to kill and . . . That doesn't leave the host any happy outcome, does it?'

'Not unless you've got a banishment spell and can confine the host safely. Then an exorcism will drive it out.'

James remembered the demon that was banished in the basement below Lucky Pete's in Krondor. 'I've seen a banishment. Is it like that?'

'Something like that. You have to bind the human host, to protect it, then a priest can banish the demon and save the host. Some of the better-trained members of the Order of the Shield of the Weak can, as well.' He lowered his voice a little. 'Though truth to tell, they're a fair lot for just bashing first and asking questions second.'

James mulled this over, then asked, 'Anyone in the city with the skills?'

'Certainly,' said Eli. 'My friend the prior to start with, and maybe three or four others.'

'That's good to know,' said James, standing.

'One more thing about the exorcism,' added Eli.

'What?'

'If the demon's been inside too long, there's not much of the host left. The body may be fine, but the mind . . .' He grimaced. 'Living as a drooling, mindless creature, or death; I'll leave it to you to decide which is the kinder fate.' He paused, then added, 'And there was one story of a demon killed by a Knight-Adamant of Sung; it possessed the head of a very powerful family in Kesh by taking over a merchant who then mysteriously died while serving the son of the noble, who some time later died alone in his father's company. Caused a stir when the knight stormed in and killed the father, but when people saw the demon flee – big cloud of smoke and stench – then considered the untimely deaths . . .' He shrugged. 'But we're still left with the why of it, aren't we? What did the demon want?'

James looked at Brother Eli and said, 'Thank you. When this is done, I'm going to send you something, but for the moment this will have to do.' He reached into his belt pouch and pulled out a gold coin and handed it to the monk.

'A sovereign,' said Eli with a smile. 'Not a small gift.'

'There'll be more. One more thing. Tell me, why is there no organization to the thieves here? Nothing like the Ragged Brotherhood or the Mockers?'

'Long story,' said Eli. 'But the short of it is, over the years the governors of Durbin and the Captains of the Coast were pretty brutal in killing off the competition, as it were. So the thieves and bashers, the whores and pickpockets, well, they just go it alone or find a patron.'

'Patron?'

'A particularly powerful merchant who puts the word out that this lad or that girl is his, and anyone who messes with them has a price to pay. Each ship's captain, each bandit chief, they have their boys and girls around the city. You thinking of reaching out from Krondor for the Mockers?'

James laughed. 'Let's say I'm not on the best of terms with my former brethren.' He thought for a minute, then added, 'Can you find me a couple of smart, trustworthy lads?'

'I can.'

'One's a fast rider?'

'As well.'

'Good,' said James. 'First I'd like a lad to amble over to the Jade Monkey and poke around a bit. He's not to say anything about who sent him, but just look around. I want to know if business has returned to normal and the girl known as Jade is well, then he's to seek out my companions, or at least rumour of their whereabouts, should he not see them at the Jade Monkey.

'Then send that rider to the oasis three days to the

south-west and pass a note to whichever Hazara-Khan noble happens to be in charge.' He glanced around. 'You have pen and parchment?'

'I do,' said the monk, indicating the desk.

James handed him a half-dozen silver coins, then took up pen and parchment and scribbled a long note, then folded it and folded it again. 'Your rider needs to leave now and with all haste get this to the family of Lord Hazara-Khan at the Bal-Shala oasis.'

Eli stood up. 'I shall see to it at once, young sir. And where will I find you should the boy encounter your friends?'

James said, 'If you have no objections, I'll wait here a while.'

The monk nodded and James lay back down on the bed, trying to find some ease for the still-aching shoulder and sharp splinter wounds, despite the stench in the hovel. As sleep sought to overtake him, he redoubled his vow to send new bedding to Brother Eli as soon as possible.

• CHAPTER THIRTEEN •

Realization

William sank down in the doorway. He had left the Jade Monkey and tried as best he could to determine where Jazhara had been taken. After nearly an hour of wandering the dark streets in a cloak he had purloined from an unconscious drunk outside an inn, he had reached the point of despair. He had no clue as to where James was, nor to whom to turn. The city watch was corrupt beyond imagining and James carried the gold for the party. They would refuse to lift a finger to help without a significant bribe.

He thought of going to the governor, but like James, distrusted the man and thought he might even be party to the assault. His mind raced but he couldn't come up with a coherent thought, let alone a plan.

He was now opposite the entrance to the Jade Monkey, crouched in a doorway in the pre-dawn gloom, not trusting it to be safe to re-enter. His attackers might have returned. So, lacking a better plan, he decided to wait until sunrise before entering, and perhaps until he saw James return, if he also wasn't abducted.

He was wondering if, once the sun was up, perhaps he might return to the rooftop behind the inn to see if there was any sign of James, then thought it likely the body of the man who died up there had been found. The city watch might be corrupt, but that wouldn't prevent them from arresting him for that man's death, should he be found anywhere near him.

What to do? William was a soldier, and if Knight-Marshal Gardan was to be taken at his word, on his way to being a fine leader of men. But he was not cut out for this skulking and plotting and creeping through dark alleys and sewers. When he was with James, he felt equal to anything, but on his own he felt a fish out of water.

He saw a boy hurrying down the street, looking around as if not wanting to be seen; then he dodged into the entrance of the Jade Monkey. That piqued William's interest.

He moved out of the shadows and glanced around. The pre-dawn was quickly lighting the street enough for him not to fear unanticipated attack, and he knew that within minutes the usual traffic of those starting their day's business would be in full flow.

He walked to the entrance and saw the boy speaking with

Gina. He saw no one else in the commons, so he entered and threw back his hood.

'William!' she exclaimed. 'You're alive!'

'James?'

'I haven't seen him.'

He saw that she had a large wet cloth pressed against the back of her head. 'Are you all right?' he asked her.

'I've had worse,' she said, 'but it's going to take a bit of time to fix things upstairs. The three thugs who came looking for you tore the place up.'

'Did you see them?'

'Didn't really see anything,' she said, wincing. 'I was vaguely aware of three men walking in, one came to the bar as if to ask me something, I turned, and the next thing I remember is waking up behind the bar with a throbbing head and a drunk next to me.'

'Are you Sir William?' the boy asked.

William sized him up. No more than ten or eleven years old, he was wearing a ragged tunic soon to be too small as he was growing: his trousers were cut off below the knees. He was barefoot, with unkempt dark hair, brown eyes, and uncertain skin colour under all that dirt, though William suspected it was lightish brown. 'Who are you?' he asked.

The boy didn't give him a name but merely said, 'I am one seeking you and the Lady Jazhara.'

'I am seeking her as well,' said William.

'Is the lady not with you?'

'No,' said William in disgust. He felt it a personal failure that Jazhara had been taken, and his fear of losing her kept rising up to send him into uncharacteristic panic.

'Then you alone must come, sir!' said the boy.

'Come where?'

'Brother Eli, a monk of Ban-ath, he seeks you out.'

Gina and William glanced at one another and almost simultaneously said, 'Ban-ath?'

'That means James,' William said.

'I'll be here should she return,' said Gina.

William thought it best not to correct her presumption that Jazhara was out somewhere without him, rather than mention her abduction. He wasn't sure why, but he thought it best that people in Durbin didn't know the daughter of one of the more important nobles in the Empire had been captured. He would wait until James decided what to do. James was the more senior member of the prince's court, and William knew his own judgement at this moment was entirely untrustworthy.

'Lead on,' said William to the boy.

As the morning markets opened and the stalls and shops were unshuttered, the boy half-walked, half-ran through the thickening crowd, with William following close behind. While it was not a sprawling city like Krondor, Durbin was densely packed once the sun rose, and soon they were both forced to slow their progress.

In less than a half-hour they reached the hovel behind the run-down shrine and found the monk sitting beside a sleeping James. William rushed over as the monk rose to greet him but before he could speak, William gripped James's shoulder.

With a grunt of pain James sat up, his dagger in his hand. Only a last-minute recognition kept him from slicing William's throat.

'Don't ever do that again, Willy.'

'What?' asked William, taken aback.

'He dislocated his left shoulder and you just grabbed it,' Brother Eli supplied helpfully.

'Oh, sorry,' said William.

'Brother Eli,' said the monk, introducing himself. 'A servant of Ban-ath.'

'William of Krondor, Knight-Lieutenant in the prince's palace guard.' To James he said, 'They've taken Jazhara!'

James stared at him. 'Who is "they"?'

'I don't know. We heard a crash in your room. By the time I opened your door, the window had been broken outward and when I went to look, someone seized her from behind. Another man attacked me and I broke his neck—'

'Good,' said James.

'—and when I gathered my wits I went back inside and found Gina unconscious. I searched for Jazhara, but found no trace of her.'

'I know where she is,' said James with certainty.

'Where?'

'At the governor's palace.'

'Are you certain?'

'Yes.'

'What do we do?'

James was silent for a moment, then said, 'I've sent a message to Jazhara's kinsmen at the oasis at Bal-Shala telling them she's been taken and to come to Durbin with all haste. But it will take another five or six days to get them here.'

William's eyes widened. 'But they are not at Bal-Shala.'

'Where are they?' asked James, rising from the cot.

'They're already en route from Bal-Shala. When we camped at the wadi, Jazhara sent along one of the Izmalis to her uncle's people, asking them to come to Durbin. She expected we'd find the governor somehow mixed up in this mess.'

'How long ago was this?'

'She dispatched him the day we arrived. The Hazara-Khan retinue should be here tomorrow morning, evening at the latest.'

'I don't think we have that much time,' said James. 'They took Jazhara either because she makes a good bargaining token with Lord Hazara-Khan, or because she's a magic-user and of particular danger to them. If it's the first, she'll be safe for the time being, but if it's the second . . .' James left unsaid that in the second case she'd be dead already. He saw the concern in William's face and said, 'I think they're making her a hostage. Else why abduct her instead of slipping a dagger in her back?'

William nodded.

'If I had those Izmalis here instead of with her uncle's people—'

'They're not with her family,' said William. 'They're still

at the wadi. Jazhara decided having them close at hand might prove useful.'

James was suddenly animated. 'If you weren't in love with that woman, I would be!' He fell silent for a moment, calculating. 'If you ride now, how soon can you be back with them?'

'If I take two horses, a little after sunset, I should think,' answered William.

'Leave now.' James pulled out his purse. He tossed it to William and said, 'I'll get into the palace and see if I can keep her safe until you arrive. Stop here first, and if I have her, we'll be in this room. If I don't, come to the palace as fast as you can. Don't be polite. Just kick down the door and come in and find us.'

William didn't need to be urged to take action; he grabbed the purse out of the air, turned and ran towards the nearest stable, nearly knocking over half a dozen people.

James flexed his injured shoulder, stretching away stiffness.

'How do you plan to get inside?' asked Brother Eli.

James looked at him with raised eyebrows, but said nothing.

After a moment, Brother Eli smiled. 'Stupid question.'

Breaking into a guarded building was nothing new for James. It was more problematic breaking into one in daylight, but while it was a rare occurrence, it was also nothing new. Breaking into one guarded by men who might be Nighthawks had but one precedent, one he'd rather forget, for it had almost cost him his life.

James had spent an hour reacquainting himself with the environs of the governor's palace. He had explored it several times while watching for the emergence of Nighthawks and just wanted one more look before committing himself to going in. He worried about Jazhara's safety, but prudence dictated a studied approach: he wouldn't do her much good dead.

Now he was walking through the heart of the city, blending in as best he could while he pondered. Another concern nagged at him: there seemed to have been two groups of Nighthawks, or rather a band of real Nighthawks and a group of false ones when he had been dealing with the Crawler's agents in Krondor. Puzzling over the apparent desire on the part of the Crawler to cast blame on the Nighthawks for his agents' handiwork, Jimmy decided the likelihood was that the men in black he had seen riding out from the governor's palace were not true assassins.

Which didn't make them any less a murdering bunch of thugs. But there was less of a chance of reprisals from the Nighthawks if he put paid to them. At least, James hoped so. Then he mentally corrected himself: there was no true Crawler. Still, he thought, even though the crime lord was a fiction, it was a fiction created by the governor or someone high up in his palace, so for the sake of keeping his thoughts in order, he assigned the label 'Crawler' to whoever that might be.

Now urgency was starting to outweigh caution. From what

he had noted when he had visited the palace, he judged the most likely access to where Jazhara was being kept would be the stables nearest the gate from which the four black riders had emerged. There, or somewhere nearby.

His logic was based on two factors: for everyone in the governor's palace to be part of some dark plot was unlikely – too many servants and minor officials were in and out of there every day, as well as merchants, vendors, carters, wagon drivers, and errand boys – and wherever the black riders and Jazhara were, it would be somewhere most servants and none of the nobility and functionaries would wander: the stables.

James had two avenues of approach: either through the main gate which, given the daily traffic in and out of the palace, wouldn't prove difficult; or over the wall. The problem was, either choice had drawbacks.

He weighed his options and finally devised a plan. His delight at his own ingenuity made him almost forget Jazhara's plight for a moment, but only for a moment. Ignoring his sore shoulder and itching back, he hurried off into the city.

Two hours later a rider garbed in expensive robes leading a magnificent stallion approached the entrance to the governor's stables. He dismounted and banged loudly on the gate.

It had taken James nearly half an hour of haggling with Jacob the moneylender to get his hands on the sum sufficient to buy the best horse in Durbin. He had basically been forced to promise Jacob he could safely return to Krondor once James returned, and that he would protect him from the

Mockers. By the time James left with the money, he was surprised Jacob hadn't asked for a parade down the central boulevard of the city to the prince's palace, with a royal reception and lunch thrown in for good measure.

After James had banged on the gate a few more times, the viewing plate slid aside and a face peered at him. 'What do you want?' demanded the servant.

'I bring the governor's new horse.'

'New horse? I know of none such.'

'Are you the governor?' asked James in as condescending a tone as he could muster. He spoke passable Keshian but was affecting an odd accent just to add to the confusion.

'No—'

'Then open the bloody gate and take this fractious creature to the stable! I merely carry out my master's orders.'

There was a moment of deliberation, then the peek-through slid shut and another moment passed, and then the gate opened. James led both horses through and handed the reins of the stallion to the servant. As soon as the stallion felt unsure hands on the reins, he began to pull away and the servant nearly lost his grip.

'By the gods, you fool!' shouted James, raising the level of noise and excitement. 'Don't let go, else you'll be chasing him through the city for days!' He reached out and took the reins, then handed his own horse's reins to the servant. 'Show me to the stable and I'll put him in a stall.'

The servant, now very flustered, nodded and said, 'This way.'

James watched as the man awkwardly shut the gate behind him while holding on to James's mount. He was so distracted he hadn't thought to hand the reins back to James while he did it.

Good, thought James. He wanted the man to be so preoccupied with what was taking place that he wouldn't notice who James was. If all went according to plan, James would have Jazhara out of there and safely hidden somewhere by the time William and the Izmalis returned. Then they'd wait for her family and put right this mess in the governor's household. But while he wanted all this done, he didn't want too many people taking a good look at him, certainly not when he was clearly the prince's man in Durbin, for he intended to return here, build up what he had started at the Jade Monkey and move on, into the Empire, constructing a network that his sons – should he have any – and his grandsons – if he had any of those – would continue to use in service to the Kingdom.

Inside the stable it took James less than a minute to render the servant unconscious after the stallion had been put in a stall. He struck him from behind, then pried open his mouth and poured in the contents of a small vial. The man would sleep for the rest of the day and then the night, and awake tomorrow with a massive headache. It was unkind, but better than killing him, and James needed to guarantee he didn't awake and raise the alarm before he found Jazhara.

James quickly removed the small burr he had put under the ornate saddle that was part of the 'governor's gift' and the horse instantly calmed down. 'Forgive me, boy,' said James, patting him, and got a reassuring snort in return.

James had no intention of leaving as valuable an animal as this one behind; he needed a second horse so Jazhara could ride out of here. He judged that once he got her into this stable, assuming there was no immediate pursuit, it would take him less than two minutes to ride to the gate, open it and be through.

He positioned both horses so they could be easily and quickly mounted, then looked around. He spied a door in the rear wall and, remembering the layout of the palace from within and without, judged it likely to be his best choice. From where it stood, it would either be a pantry door or a door to stairs leading down. The latter turned out to be the case and James quickly hurried down the stairs.

At the bottom he listened and when he heard no sounds, he peered into a corridor. There was a door to his right, which he dismissed as being too near the outer wall to be more than a cupboard or small room, and a long hall off to his left, illuminated by a lone torch in an iron holder affixed to the wall. He moved down the hall.

James decided this area looked as much like a dungeon as a pantry or storage area. The doors were all of heavy wood with massive locks, and there were slides to peer through. He peered into one such but it was dark.

He listened. No sound was a mixed blessing. It meant he was unlikely to encounter anyone unexpectedly, but it also meant he was no closer to finding Jazhara than he had been before arriving in the palace. At the far end of the hallway James hesitated, for it branched left and right, but only for a moment. Keeping his orientation relative to the palace above was second nature to him. He turned the corner and was halfway down the corridor when a door behind him swung open and he turned, just as a large man in black clothing emerged and saw him. He shouted something inarticulate but angry. James realized he had no choice in the matter. There was nowhere to run.

He drew his belt-knife and charged, driving his shoulder into the man's stomach before he could draw his sword. The fashion in which he took him off his feet told James this was no true Nighthawk, which answered one question for him.

The mythical Crawler's crew had nothing to do with the real Nighthawks.

The two men went down in a heap, with James on top. He was just drawing back his dagger when he sensed another man behind him. That moment's hesitation prevented him from killing the man beneath him, and before he could protect himself, a heavy blow to the side of his head sent him spinning into darkness.

• CHAPTER FOURTEEN •

Confrontation

JAMES AWOKE IN PAIN.

He was suspended in the air, shackled to heavy chains that were bolted to the ceiling and floor. The first thing he realized as he became conscious was that his shoulder was in agony. Then he realized his head was throbbing.

Jazhara stood before him smiling. 'Are you . . .?' he began, groggily, then realized she was free. 'Get me down,' he whispered.

'No need to whisper, Sir James,' she answered, and instantly he knew he wasn't speaking to Jazhara.

A single torch in a sconce on the wall behind James threw deep shadows into the corners of the room, and his field of vision was limited. He found he was sweating.

'No one can hear you scream,' 'Jazhara' said.

James knew he had found the demon. Or rather, she had found him.

'Lady Shandra?' he asked.

'You are a clever one, aren't you?' she said. 'My previous host.'

'What happened to her?' asked James.

With a tilt of her hand, the demon occupying Jazhara's body indicated a corner behind and to the left of James. He craned his neck over his shoulder but all he could see were two pairs of legs extending out of the gloom: one, as far as he could see, male; the other female.

'The governor and his wife?' asked James. He kept a lock-pick in his right sleeve, but hanging from these chains made it impossible to reach. If he was to survive long enough for help to arrive, he first had to remain alive.

'She was useful, for a while, but this body has so much more to offer,' said the demon. 'Though her mind has retreated behind some sort of barrier.' She cocked her head to one side as if listening to another voice. 'With your kind, I have their memories and know all they know within minutes, but Jazhara's magic has shielded her. I've possessed a dozen before Lady Shandra and it was always amusing to have them there, with me, tucked away in a corner of their own body, unable to do anything but watch me and scream. Sometimes they'd be driven mad, but other times they would rage, beg, threaten. It's very entertaining. To me, it's much like your music. So many variations, so many different tunes. There was the idiot who thought summoning me would do a service for his god, and then a travelling merchant with a great deal of gold. After I killed off his entire retinue except for the strongest warrior, I took the warrior and killed the merchant.' She smiled and James could not believe a face so familiar to him could suddenly become so alien, so evil. 'It took a while, but my master wanted to do little but sow discord, and for a while random bloodshed was amusing. But when I managed to take Lady Shandra while she was out shopping, then I realized I had learned enough about human politics to know that starting a major war would be of far more service to my master than what I had been doing thus far. So, here we are.' She waved her hand around as if encompassing all of the governor's palace.

James felt sick to his inner core. He didn't know if distracting her might somehow give Jazhara any help, but he felt he had nothing to lose. 'So why aren't I dead?' he asked.

'I need you,' said the demon. 'At least for a little while longer.'

'Why?'

'You'll see.' The demon's mannerisms were reminiscent of Lady Shandra, at least from what James remembered from the one time they had met.

'Why kill the governor?' asked James.

'When I leave a host there's not much of a mind left behind, and having his very alert and clever wife suddenly become bereft of reason would be difficult to explain. There are illnesses that leave a healthy, mature woman suddenly slack-jawed and drooling, but a good healing cleric might find traces of my being there. Moreover, once they realized there was no healing spell known that could restore her mind, the thought that this might be a simple brain seizure would pass and they'd start seeking other causes. I do not need people guessing I'm here.' She grinned. 'But a brutal murder by a rogue agent of the Prince of Krondor . . .' she smiled and there was nothing humorous or warm in that expression, 'now that could prove very useful. A serious war between Kesh and the Kingdom would certainly take attention away for a while.' She glanced around the room, as if waiting for something.

'Away from what?'

The face that had been Jazhara's lost its smile. 'You've been a thorn in our side, Jimmy the Hand.'

'Whose side?'

'I serve one who has very long-term goals here, Jimmy. And you've managed to thwart him three times.' She sighed theatrically. 'The fool who attacked Arutha at Sarth sent a thing, a monster with no mind to speak of, the most primitive construct; the summonings at the Tomb of the Hopeless; and those in Krondor. Poor attempts at best. But when this one mad warlock up in the mountains thought he'd summon a demon to bargain for long life . . .' She grinned and there was no trace of Jazhara in her eyes. 'My master dispatched me instead of the annoying little imps that usually answer those calls.' She laughed. 'I merely waited inside his circle, invisible, until he foolishly stepped inside to see what he had done wrong. Once the ring was broken, he was mine!'

'What do you want?' asked James.

She shrugged. 'He whom I serve is so far above me, I only do his bidding, never asking his reasons or questioning his motives. I am but one of many who serve him. My mandate is to cause havoc, to bring chaos, and keep you humans distracted.'

'Distracted from what?'

She wagged her finger at him. 'It is what it is. You will die never knowing.'

'Who is your master?'

She shook her head, saying nothing. 'Perhaps one day you'll find out. Perhaps not. It's immaterial. At first, we tried to keep you alive. I thought it would not do to have Prince Arutha's agent in Kesh turning up dead in Durbin, nor drawing attention to the Crawler, here. He was supposed to be a distant and mythical personage, keeping your filthy Mockers off balance. When you balked our attempts to summon my brothers into Krondor, we conspired to keep you there, while we . . .' That unnerving smile returned. 'It doesn't matter what we are doing here. It only matters that we succeed. Now, we will wait for my agents to find your other companion and ensure that he is part of this grisly tale.'

She was silent and still for a moment, as if listening to something. 'Jazhara returning to Krondor with a tale of betrayal and murder, a plot to throw discredit upon Arutha, that will prove beyond any doubt her loyalty to him. We will ensure that Kesh sees her as part of the murder plot, paint her a traitor and further drive a wedge between these two nations.'

She was silent again while James waited, struggling to contrive a way out of this situation. He knew things looked hopeless, but life had so far taught him hope only died with surrender. He might be flung from the highest tower on this world, but he would be thinking of a way to escape until the moment he struck the ground.

Suddenly Jazhara closed her eyes tightly and let out a sound of pain, as if struck by a blinding headache. She opened her eyes and for a brief instant looked around in confusion. 'James . . .?' she whispered.

'Jazhara?'

'Don't let her . . . use me.' Suddenly her eyes closed tightly, then she stood upright as if shaking off the pain. 'The little minx fights back!' She was motionless for a long moment. At last she opened her eyes again and sighed. 'Ah, there. Jazhara's defences weaken. Her will is strong, but mine is stronger.'

Time dragged on. James tried to wrest information out of the demon, against the faint possibility he might somehow survive and put it to good use. She was adamant in not revealing anything of her mission or who she served. In the end, all he was left with was that she must be stopped: she could not be allowed to travel to Krondor disguised as Arutha's magic-advisor. He knew what the next, inevitable step must be.

'The death of the Governor of Durbin at the hands of

the prince's advisor will bring problems enough,' he said. 'The death of the Prince of Krondor at the hands of the niece of one of the most powerful nobles in the Empire will start the war you seek.'

Laughter erupted from the demon. 'You are almost as clever as they said you were.' She looked at James and he was sure he caught a gleam of horror behind her eyes. 'The death of Lord Hazara-Khan's niece at the hands of the Prince of Krondor as she attempts to kill him and his family, that will be even better – it will bring what we desire. When Arutha declares war without the King's leave, not even his brother will say nay.' She looked down coyly. 'Especially when the prince is mad with grief over the foul murder of his beloved wife and children.'

James recoiled. 'You'll kill Anita and the children, then possess Arutha,' he said, sick at the thought of such an evil plan.

She nodded. 'By then Jazhara's mind will be that of a simpering child. She will not be able to defend herself when Arutha kills her with his bare hands. It's all a matter of timing. Just kill the children first, then the princess before Arutha turns up. I think perhaps as they are sleeping and she thinks everything in her world is perfect.'

James hung from his chains, unable to think of any way to prevent the most horrifying plot he could imagine – the murder of the five people in the world he loved the most, which would in turn engender the biggest catastrophe ever to face the Kingdom.

'Ah,' the demon said, 'I believe your friend is coming.'

'Willy will never believe you,' said James. 'You don't have enough knowledge to feign being Jazhara.'

'He will believe I am distraught over the need to kill you,' she countered, 'and in a few days I will have torn down these barriers in Jazhara's mind and will have all her knowledge.'

'She'll find a way to prevent that!'

The demon laughed. 'She may as well be dead, James. If you had a powerful cleric with the right knowledge and had me dislodged last night . . . perhaps she would have emerged intact. She is using whatever magic and mental strength she has left to battle me, seeking to wrest back control, but she is losing and now she's reduced to just keeping me away from her memories, but those defences are wearing thinner by the moment. Even if you could banish me now, she would be no more than a shadow of what she was. Oh, she'd have most of her memories, and her magic, but she would be a frightened little girl compared to the woman you knew.'

James struggled. 'I'll see you in hell!'

The demon laughed. 'I've been there. It really isn't so bad if you're used to it.'

The sounds of struggle echoed from outside the door, the clash of swords, the clatter of boot heels on stone, and suddenly the door was thrown open.

The demon waved her hand and before the door swung fully wide, the chains parted and James fell to the floor. He groaned in pain as he struck the stones and shook his head as William rushed in and saw the two of them, Jazhara cowering in the far corner, standing over the bodies of the governor and his wife, and James crouched on the floor, covered in blood, looking like some sort of animal.

'Willy!' James shouted.

'Willy!' shouted the demon. 'It's a demon: it's taken possession of James!'

William stood motionless for a moment. James looked at him through puffy eyes. 'Willy, don't believe her. That's not Jazhara!'

The demon hurried across the room, tears running down her cheeks. 'Willy, don't believe him. He has James's memories. He will kill us when he gets the chance, then he'll kill the prince!'

For what seemed an eternity William stood transfixed. He looked first at Jazhara, then at James. He weighed what his eyes beheld and knew he must make a murderous decision. He stepped toward James, and the demon came to stand behind him, her hand on his shoulder, as if seeking his protection.

Three Izmalis came into the room and stood behind William. They hesitated, unsure of what was going on. William looked at James, pain etched across his features, and he asked, 'Must I?'

'Yes!' shouted the demon in William's ear. 'Kill him!'

James could barely answer. He whispered, 'Yes.' Taking a deep breath, he said, 'Kill us both.'

William hesitated for one moment longer.

Then over William's shoulder, James saw 'Jazhara' close

her eyes as if in sudden pain and grab her forehead. Tears welled up and she let out a whimper. 'William . . .'

The tone of her voice was enough to make William hesitate, then he heard her say, 'I'm . . . lost . . . my love . . .'

With a scream of anger, the demon shook off Jazhara's last attempt to defy her and shouted, 'Kill him!'

For a long moment William seemed frozen, unable to move. Then suddenly he reversed his sword and, thrusting it behind him, plunged it into the stomach of the woman he loved.

Feeling the bite of steel, the demon screamed. As she crumpled to the floor, she asked, 'How . . .?'

'Jazhara would never call me "Willy",' he answered simply.

The demon threw back her head as the Izmalis drew their swords, not understanding what had happened, and then a cloud of foul, green smoke erupted from her mouth. They stepped back in horror, but William knelt, and when the smoke was gone, he raised Jazhara up and held her tightly.

After a moment, Jazhara's eyes focused on William's face and she whispered, 'Thank you, my love.' And then her head lolled to one side.

William stood there holding her lifeless body until James put an arm around his shoulder, helped him lower Jazhara gently to the floor, then led his friend away.

• CHAPTER FIFTEEN •

Krondor

ARUTHA LISTENED SILENTLY.

James finished the report, and Arutha was silent for a long moment, then said, 'An ill thing, despite us putting an end to this Crawler business and the demon hoax behind it.'

William had stood motionless, his face a mask, while James had described the entire incident.

After killing the demon, they had waited until Jazhara's kinsmen arrived. A cousin, one of Lord Hazara-Khan's sons, installed himself as temporary Governor of Durbin until an appointment from the city of Great Kesh arrived. They had listened to the complete recounting of events and, upon seeing the governor and his wife's bodies as well as that of Jazhara, and the dead would-be Nighthawks who had opposed the Izmalis and William, as well as hearing testimony from servants about the odd goings-on around the palace for the previous year or more, had reached the conclusion that things had occurred just as James had testified – his own beaten countenance had further persuaded them that the story was true.

It was a long and unhappy journey home from Durbin for James and William. Long hours of silence passed as they either stayed in their cabins or walked the decks of the ship hired to take them to Krondor. Killing the only woman he had truly loved hung heavy around William's neck like a chain of iron, even though he knew it was the only choice he could have made. No matter how much James had tried to convince him that Jazhara had already been lost before he had arrived, he still could not rid himself of the memory of plunging his blade into her stomach.

At last Arutha said, 'William, would you care to visit your family?'

William hesitated. 'I'd prefer to return to duty as soon as possible, Highness.'

Arutha studied his face, then nodded once. 'Dismissed. Report to Gardan.'

William saluted and departed.

When they were alone, Arutha pushed his chair away from his desk and said, 'Do you think he'll get over it?'

James shook his head. 'No. Eventually, he would have let go of whatever guilt he felt about Talia – he was actually dealing with that well. But Jazhara . . .' James let silence fall for a full minute, then added, 'Had we not reached the Black Lake and found Silverthorn . . .'

Arutha said nothing, remembering when his wife Anita had hovered at the edge of death, her life sustained only by magic, as he and James and others had searched in the north for the plant that would provide the cure. He closed his eyes and pinched the bridge of his nose, as if willing away the haunting fear that they might never find the antidote and the consequence of failure he had carried with him from the moment she had been struck by the assassin's crossbow bolt until the moment she was saved. It had been the worst time he could remember. Finally, he took a deep breath and said, 'He'll carry this one the rest of his life.'

James said, 'I'm Willy's friend. What do I do?'

'You just continue as his friend, Jimmy. In this he is alone.'

Arutha stood and walked around his desk to stand before the former street-boy who had become one of his most valuable associates, and a close friend. 'Sometimes all we can do is carry a thing, Jimmy. Sometimes the best we can do is not let that thing slow us down or deter us, but there are burdens we *never* put down.' The prince paused, looking James in the eyes. 'As his friends, all we can do is to help keep him going. For if he lets this stop him, he'll never start again. He will find his life and purpose, and one day even some happiness, but this is something that will always mark him.'

James could only nod, knowing he was right.

Arutha added, 'I think it best if we keep our young knight-lieutenant busy for a while.'

James smiled. 'He'll never admit it, but as much as he enjoys being a soldier, there's a little bit of a rogue inside Willie, too.'

Arutha returned the smile, ruefully. 'Speaking of rogues, I'm going to recall Locklear.'

James laughed. 'If anyone can cheer Willy up, Locky's the lad.'

'I'm thinking of keeping you three close by. Let's just say I may have some difficult tasks ahead, and if you can keep Locky from causing too much trouble, I think he would be a useful addition to your . . . whatever you're calling your merry band.'

'No name, Sire,' said James.

'Are you building me a spy network, Jimmy?'

'The best I can, Highness.'

Arutha's expression revealed he was caught between amusement and worry. Finally he said, 'If you get too sure of yourself, remember Jazhara.'

James's expression turned sombre. 'I will, Highness.'

'The game you play often has a high price. I fear, too high at times.'

'But we must play, mustn't we, Highness?'

'I fear we must.' Arutha sighed. 'Go, nose around the city and see what has happened while you've been away. I know you're itching to, and you always seem to turn up something useful. I'm going to pen a message to Pug; even if he's heard of Jazhara's death from other sources, I need to tell him how sorry we are.' With an almost pained expression, he added,

'Then I must request he send us another magician.'

'Whoever he sends, I'll do my best to make sure this never happens again, Highness.'

Arutha nodded and gestured that Jimmy had his permission to withdraw.

James bowed slightly, and left the prince's office. He walked briskly down the hall. William would do well under Gardan's care for the time being. And within a few weeks Locklear would return and things would prove lively.

Despite his sadness at Jazhara's death, he knew that he had uncovered one more piece of a very large and important puzzle. There was something out there that was a danger to them all, and James was determined to solve that puzzle.

He hurried through the palace, eager to return to the haunts and dives of the city he loved best.